The Bodyguard

Bella Reves

Published by Bella Reves, 2023.

THE BODYGUARD

First edition. December 4, 2023.

Copyright © 2023 Bella Reves.

ISBN: 979-8223436621

Written by Bella Reves.

Table of Contents

This book is dedicated to my parents, who always encouraged me to follow my dreams. I'm sure they hoped I would dream of being a doctor, but alas, I dreamt of this instead.

Chapter 1

Kacey

I gripped the sides of the sink like it would somehow keep me tethered to the earth. The bass from the club was unbearably loud, even in the dimly lit bathroom, and I could feel it vibrating through my ribcage. It definitely wasn't helping the nausea I was currently willing myself to push through. The last...whatever that shot was, was not agreeing with the other five - no, wait was it six? - I'd already had that night.

God, how did I get here?

As if on cue, my phone buzzed in my pocket. I pulled it out, nearly dropping it in the sink in my haste. It was a text from Alexis, my wonderful, if somewhat demanding, manager.

Post!!!

Succinct and to the point, as if she instinctively knew that I would be too sloshed to handle full sentences. A curse on whoever had proposed the last round of shots. Okay, that may have been me.

Fighting a wave of nausea, I gave myself a bleary once over in the mirror, thankful for the club's terrible lighting, and ran a quick hand through my hair to give it a sexy 'tousled' look. With a couple of taps on my phone, the camera blinked to life.

"Hey besties!" I announced, putting on my fake, sultry smile. "My verdict on the new and gorgeous Red Velvet ultra sheer lip stain is in: It's a keeper!" I gave a little celebratory hop - not easy in heels - and immediately regretted it when my stomach did another flip and I nearly fumbled my phone. "This lip stain can hold out for a whole night of partying - even if you can't." I gave a cheeky little wink and blew a kiss at the camera, then stopped recording and sent the video to Alexis. My work done, I tossed my phone on the counter, ran into the nearest stall and promptly heaved what was left of my dignity into the toilet. As it

1

turned out, the lip stain wasn't equipped to handle that lovely aspect of partying.

I reapplied it in the mirror to hide the evidence of my Linda Blair moment and hunted down a mint from my purse. Once again presentable, I braced myself and walked back out into the overwhelming noise of the club.

My group was still over by the same table, all engrossed in their phones. They'd had the decency to not abandon me at least. Jasmine looked up when I reached them and gave me a brief once-over, eyes narrowed. Jasmine was a model - strictly high-fashion - and influencer, and she could be a bit overbearing when it came to her appearance, and the appearance of everyone around her.

"What were you doing, fucking the bartender?" Jasmine sniffed, taking in my rumpled dress and scuffed knee from when I dove for the toilet.

"Obviously" I smirked, trying not to snarl. At least I had managed to avoid getting puke on my dress. Luckily in this crowd, being a bit slutty was acceptable as long as you weren't openly trashy, so Jasmine just grimaced and went back to her phone. Flipping my hair over my shoulder, I settled in beside my actual friend Layla, who had been watching the exchange like it was a tennis match.

"Can we leave?" I begged her, leaning in close so the rest of the table couldn't hear. Not that it was hard to have a private conversation in a club, the music was so loud and everyone was so self-absorbed I could have yelled it and not gotten a second glance.

"Worried your bartender will come back for round two?" Layla smirked. She was obnoxiously pretty like Jasmine, but way less bitchy and full of herself, thank god. Having grown up with her, you'd think I'd be jealous of how gorgeous she was, but Layla was the kind of pretty that was beyond jealousy. You couldn't be jealous of Layla any more than an ant could be jealous of a god.

"Of course" I replied, my smile coming in a bit forced as the bass from the music started to rattle around in my skull. "You know that no one can get enough of this." I made a rather crude gesture towards my crotch, which earned me another dirty look from Jasmine. Clearly, she was the life of the party.

"Alright, let's go before Jasmine slits your throat." Layla laughed. "I'll order the Uber." I nodded and put my back against the table, leaning against it for support. I watched the people dancing and drinking around us, oblivious and happy in their own little lives. I also caught glimpses of other solo clubbers here and there - mainly guys cruising for single women. They looked like sharks waiting to smell blood in the water. My eyes stopped on one man in particular, and the hairs on the back of my neck prickled. He was partially obscured in shadow near the back of the club, but somehow I knew he was staring right at me.

I'd been getting that feeling for weeks now. Out of nowhere my stomach would sink and I'd get this overwhelming sense that someone was watching me. I guess I was just getting even more self-absorbed as I got older. Plus, who'd be watching me when there was usually a table of models nearby? They just naturally drew the eye with their miles-long legs and overall sunny dispositions.

"All set, one last selfie for the 'gram?" Layla announced, jolting me out of my drunken reveries. I turned back to the table, forcing my last smile of the evening. "Of course!"

Layla held out her phone and crouched considerately to make up for our height difference. Even in heels, I didn't reach the collarbone of my friend, whose stature would have an Amazonian Queen doing a double-take. After the picture was snapped and approved, we went through the perfunctory 10 minutes of "Oh my god you can't leave yet!" and "Bitch, you had better tag me in those pics this time". We managed to extricate ourselves and wade through the undulating masses to get to the front door.

Sinking into the back seat of a blue 4-door something or other, I closed her eyes and let the ringing in my ears settle down while Layla made sure the driver had the right directions. The car took off with a lurch that kicked off a new wave of nausea, and I cracked my window to coax some fresh air into the already stuffy vehicle. Layla was busy typing on her phone - she still handled most of her own social media curation. I was ever-thankful that I had foisted that aspect of my life onto Alexis, who seemed to actually enjoy that part of the job. Honestly, I would pay triple what I was paying now as long as it meant avoiding being responsible for coming up with hashtags, picking filters and responding 'Omg LOVE you!' to all the various comments that piled up on my posts. Truthfully, I barely even looked at my own pages anymore. My real friends had my direct number, and anyone else who tried to contact me was first screened by Alexis. She was like a walking, talking spam filter. I made a mental note to order Alexis one of those fancy cookie bouquets, and then immediately regretted the thoughts of food in my current state.

I managed to keep from puking until we reached my condo, a heroic feat that saved Layla's Uber rating, but cost my condo building a potted plant. Whatever, it was an ugly plant anyway. I purposefully avoided the disapproving glare of the doorman as Layla escorted me upstairs. Once we reached my fifth-floor condo, I gave up all pretence of dignity and stumbled to the bathroom, stripping off my clothes and shedding the last remnants of the awful night.

Chapter 2

Kacey

At some point, Layla had covered me in a blanket and left a bottle of water on the floor beside my face. One day, I will figure out how to get her nominated for sainthood. Some time in the early morning hours, the floor had stopped spinning and I had drifted into a fitful sleep on the fluffy white bathmat my mother had insisted was 'tacky' and 'outdated'. Well, the joke was on her, because it was perfect for a drunken bathroom sleep.

In your face, Mom.

Once I was able to stand without doubling over, I hobbled to the shower and tried to wash off the layer of grime that had somehow built up on my skin over the course of the night. As soon as I was finished scrubbing the last of my makeup off - Goddamn was that lip stain stubborn! - another wave of hangover exhaustion washed over me. I wandered out to the kitchen for some much-needed caffeine, wrapping a towel around my waist to let my hair and my boobs air dry. I was a bit of a nudist at heart, and often wandered around my condo in various states of undress. Layla was used to the sight of my nipples first thing in the morning, it was one of the hazards of staying the night. She wasn't a modest person either, in fact, being a model, she'd probably seen more breasts at her job than most people had seen their entire lives.

Grabbing my phone off the hallway table as I walked past, I turned it back on and winced as the notifications started popping up. I'm glad I turned it off because drunk-Kacey had a tendency to get into some nasty text misadventures. I'd somehow missed 13 calls from Alexis, and there were at least 20 new unread texts. Fuck, that's what I get for passing out in the bathroom for eight hours. I quickly scanned the texts from Alexis, but they were all variations of *PICK UP YOUR FUCKING PHONE* and gave no indication of why she needed to talk.

5

That couldn't be good. Did I steal something last night? Or flash the Uber driver? The details were pretty hazy, but I'm pretty sure I had just imagined punching Jasmine in the mouth and hadn't actually done it, right?

I turned the corner into my kitchen, my nose still buried in my phone. There was an unread text from my most recent ex - oh fuck. If I had drunk texted him last night I would actually jump off my balcony. When I opened it and saw a *You up?* Followed by a picture of his very erect penis, I actually sighed in relief.

"You won't believe this Layla, Rex got a Prince Albert! I didn't know they could pierce a micro-penis." I snorted. I was just being petty, my ex's penis was actually a very reasonable size. Unfortunately, it was his micro-heart that was the problem in our relationship, that and his penchant to fuck other women behind my back.

"Kace- oh shit. You have guests hun!" Layla yelped, jumping up from the table and throwing herself in front of me.

I froze as my friend lunged at me - she, of course, looked drop-dead gorgeous and not the least bit hungover. My eyes drifted first to Layla's flustered face, then to the two people sitting at the table she'd just abandoned, and finally to the man standing against the counter. One of them I recognized right away as my manager Alexis, and the man beside her at the table was clearly some sort of policeman, judging by his uniform.

The man at the counter was a mystery, with no clear identifying uniform. He was unnecessarily handsome, and I wondered briefly if Layla had invited her latest conquest over for a booty call after tucking me in for the night. He was bulkier than the guys she'd normally hook up with though, Layla prefers the nerdier academic types - the more degrees, the better. This guy was more my type, tall with big arms and looked like he'd come out on top in a bar fight. The sexy mystery man met my gaze for a long moment, serious and unblinking. It could have been unnerving, but there was a steady softness in his brown eyes that could make me feel safe in a hurricane. His eyes shifted down ever so slightly, and then he coughed and suddenly became transfixed with the cup of coffee he was holding.

I abruptly became very aware that I was topless and still damp, and why was I just standing there staring at him?

For the love of god, cover your breasts, you idiot!

It felt like the signals from my hungover brain took a decade to finally reach my hands. I crossed my arms over my chest to try and minimize the damage, but clearly, that ship had sailed, crashed into an iceberg, and burst into flames.

"Let's find you a shirt!" Layla laughed nervously, trying to cut the tension. She had her arms out to try to shield me from view, but try as she might, it was like hiding behind a lamppost. I backed up and spun around, still covering myself. This is when my towel decided to make a bid for freedom and dropped to the floor with a deafening flop. The universe had clearly decided that today would be the first time someone spontaneously burst into flames and died from sheer embarrassment. I dropped my hands to my sides - because honestly what was the point anymore - and walked quickly to my room, Layla following behind with my towel.

I was very content to stay in my room for the rest of my life. In fact, I'd order some bricks online and they could just wall me up in there like one of those nuns I'd read about from the olden times. Unfortunately, whatever it was that had gathered everyone together in my kitchen at 9:00 a.m. on a Saturday morning was important enough that they wouldn't tell Layla without me, so unless I was ready to die of curiosity as well as embarrassment, I would need to get dressed and face them like an adult. After all my bits were reasonably covered - I wasn't actually a nun, and my body would only look this good for another five years at most - I walked back outside to the table full of people. Someone - likely Layla - had poured me a cup of coffee, and I grasped at it like a lifeline as I sat down. Layla perched on the back of the couch nearby, leaving me to face Alexis, the cop, and the hot guy drinking coffee in my kitchen.

"Sorry I missed your calls, Lexi, I turned my phone off when we got home from the club." I offered, finally breaking the awkward silence. I took a gulp of coffee and relished the heat as it slid down my throat. I could already feel a bit of life returning to my limbs. "What did I miss?"

"No, I'm sorry Kace," Alexis replied, looking down at the table. Up to this point, I'd figured I had fucked something up, maybe forgot to pay a bill or pissed someone off. But the look on Alexis's face...a cold feeling of dread started to form in the pit of my stomach.

"Ah-hem. Ms. Keeper, if I may?" The police officer interjected, when it became clear that Alexis was struggling to continue. "I'm Sergeant Jeffreys. Your manager here has made my department aware of the potential threat to your safety. Now, we take this kind of thing very seriously. While we are conducting our investigation into this matter, I want to assure you that your well-being is of top priority. So we have provided Ms. Masters with some suggestions to increase security around your home."

"Uh...what?" I looked between Sergeant Jeffreys and Alexis, desperate for context of any kind. "What do you mean a threat to my safety? Is there something wrong with the building?" I needed an IV and about a gallon more coffee, my brain was moving far too slowly to be participating in this conversation.

The look Sergeant Jeffreys gave me was one of pity, tinged with annoyance as if I was acting clueless deliberately. Not a chance, this level of stupidity was all natural. "No Ms. Keeper, the threat from your stalker. Judging from the escalating behaviour, he's getting bolder, and that's something that can no longer be ignored. Now, obviously, our first step would be a restraining order. But unfortunately, since we haven't been able to positively ID him, that's not possible at this time. In the meantime, our goal is to ensure that he doesn't get any closer to you than he already has."

I stared at the man across from me, now certain that this was the lamest practical joke ever. I waited for someone to crack a smile, but as the silence grew, so did the cold ache in my stomach. "What fucking stalker?" I asked stupidly, turning to stare at my manager. "What is he talking about Lexi?"

"I'm so sorry Kace." She whispered, unable to meet my eyes. "I thought it was nothing. You know how fans get! There are always weird accounts that take things too far, making fake wedding photos and photoshopping you with them...I always report them, block them, and delete any creepy comments. But this one account started to get really...real." She pushed a folder across the table, and I set my coffee down to grab it. Inside was my worst nightmare.

Chapter 3

Everett

What the fuck was an influencer anyway?

I was trying to go over the file for the job one more time before meeting the client but kept getting stuck on this one part. Clearly, she was big on social media, that much I understood. But what I couldn't figure out is the why of it. What was the point?

I took another sip of my coffee, cold now that I'd been sitting here for over an hour. I liked to arrive early, it gave me time to watch and learn the rhythm of a place. It was amazing what you could find out just by observing. For instance, at first glance, this condo building looked decently secure. There was a doorman stationed at the front at all times, and there was a security guard on duty by the front desk. No one could get in or out without signing in. But as I waited, a delivery driver had pulled up and gone around back, probably to a service door that bypassed the front security. Who was manning that entrance? I made a mental note to check out that entrance later today. This was the tricky part of these kinds of jobs. You had to put yourself in the mind of a stalker. And this one, I could already tell by the file, was particularly clever.

I saw my PD contact Sergeant Jefferys walking up and I stowed the file under my seat. I left my jacket in the car - It was hot enough today that I could go without it. The button-up shirt I was wearing was professional enough for a first meeting. I didn't feel the need to dress like a secret service agent, unlike some other private security guys I'd met. Sometimes it was good to draw attention and let people know that there was security nearby. But I liked the subtler approach - the element of surprise. I also fucking hated ties.

Hopping out of my car, I stretched until I felt something pop in my back. Was this what getting old felt like? I gave a small wave to the Sergeant, who nodded and waited for me to catch up. A younger woman had joined him, probably the manager who had filed the police report and hired me.

Her eyes widened when I approached, and I noticed her take a step closer to the Sergeant. I had that effect on people, my sister called it *Resting Murder Face*, but I figured it had more to do with my size than anything else. I was just over 6'3, and built like a brick shit-house according to my old commanding officer, which I think had been meant as a compliment.

I gave her a polite smile to try to put her at ease. "Ms. Masters? I'm Everett Cole, from L.T.C. Security." I flashed her my identification in case she still wasn't convinced, but the introduction seemed to do the trick. She gave me a small smile and a nod, and together the three of us walked inside and up to the fifth floor where my client lived.

The building was nice and clearly new. I noticed security cameras in the lobby, and the security guard had us sign in and pressed the button for us in the elevator since none of us had a key fob. More cameras in the elevators, but none once we reached the fifth floor. Evidently, they assumed no one could make it this far undetected. The woman who answered the door for us was not the client - I knew as much from pictures I had seen in the file. Alexis clearly knew her and took the lead, the Sergeant and I following them inside.

"This is Layla DeCroix," Alexis explained, leading us into the kitchen. The condo was huge, clearly influencing was a lucrative business. I recognized the name from the file, one of the client's known associates. I scanned the room while everyone made small talk, eyeing the doors and windows and calculating vantage points.

"-coffee?" I looked over to see everyone watching me, waiting for my answer. *Fuck, ears open Cole.* I finally noticed Layla, who was holding up a mug and a pot of coffee.

"Oh, sure thank you." I nodded. She handed me a mug and then sat down at the table with the others. Preferring to stand, I walked further into the kitchen and stood behind Sergeant Jeffreys. Leaning with my back against the counter, I had a decent view of the living room and the wall-to-wall windows that overlooked downtown.

Where was the client? Who is late to their own meeting? I frowned and took a sip of coffee - *fuck that is good* - and watched Layla argue with Alexis and the Sergeant. She was a beautiful woman, even now when she was scowling at something they'd said to her. She had an angular face, so far from human normalcy it was nearly alien, like the women in fashion magazines. It was almost surreal to see her here, arguing with a police sergeant with her hair in a messy bun and wearing sweatpants.

"We were up late working, I don't know when she'll be up. Can you just tell me what this is about? Is Kacey in trouble?" Layla snapped. I got the feeling people didn't often say no to her.

"Ms. DeCroix, please. Without Ms. Keeper here, we cannot reveal any more about the case, I'm sorry." Sergeant Jeffreys replied calmly, but he was clearly getting tired of waiting.

"You won't believe this Layla, Rex got a Prince Albert! I didn't know they could pierce a micro-penis." Everyone looked up as the woman of the hour finally entered the room. And boy, did she know how to make an entrance.

Katerina Cordelia Keeper, aka Kacey, according to the file. Unlike her ethereal friend, Kacey was decidedly human and obviously unaware that she had company. She'd just gotten out of the shower, her dark hair still damp and hanging loose around her face. Her face looked slightly raw as if she'd been rubbing it with sandpaper, and she had an imprint on her cheek like she'd slept on something hard. Her eyes met mine, and I saw surprise and confusion cross her face. My gaze dropped and I realized abruptly that she was topless, her perky breasts still glistening from the shower.

Stop staring at her tits you jackass.

Flustered, I looked into my coffee cup, but I couldn't get the image of her amazing body out of my head. It was probably burned into my retinas now.

Suddenly everyone was moving and talking at the same time. Layla had leapt up to usher her friend from the kitchen, and Sergeant Jefferys looked like he was considering retirement. I glanced up as the two women left, just in time to see the towel drop from Kacey's waist. I choked back a laugh -not at her of course, I'm not a complete asshole - but at the situation, which was basically a scene out of some bad porno. Except no one here was a handyman or a pizza delivery guy. Kacey was gorgeous, there was no denying it. The sight of her ass, so round and tight and perfect, was enough to make my cock stir. Not professional in the slightest, I really can't afford to be distracted in this line of work. I carefully adjusted myself so it wasn't noticeable, keeping my eyes safely on my coffee for now.

Layla rejoined us moments later, pouring a cup of coffee and setting it on the table. I could tell by the worry on her face that she genuinely cared for her friend. Kacey joined us a few minutes later, now dressed in a tank top and leggings, much to my disappointment. She sat down at the table, grabbing the coffee immediately. She looked surprisingly cool and collected as if she hadn't just flashed a room full of people. I couldn't help but admire her a bit for that. However, her confidence seemed to waiver as she listened to the Sergeant explain the situation, and then it morphed into pure confusion.

"What fucking stalker?" I'd seen clients who were in denial over the situation they were in before, but this was a little much. I know that it was sometimes a bit hard to believe that someone would want to hurt you, or that someone in your life could be capable of actual evil. But this guy that was stalking her wasn't exactly subtle. It was hard to interpret *I want to see the life drain from your eyes* as anything but a hostile threat.

Alexis gave Kacey a file similar to the one I had in my car, and I felt a pang of sympathy as her face blanched and she looked through the pictures and posts the sicko had made about her. She wasn't in denial, clearly, this was obviously the first time she'd seen any of these before today.

Chapter 4

Kacey

"Alexis...what the fuck." I shuffled through the photos in the file she'd given me, each one worse than the next. All of them were photos of me, with increasingly horrible captions. The older ones seemed to be screenshots from my own videos, and they said things like *'Someday we will be together'*. He'd stepped up his game in the more recent ones, somehow tracking me down in real life and taking pictures while I was completely unaware. Some were obviously from far away and he'd zoomed in, evidenced by how blurry they were. But a few were so close he could've reached out and touched me, and that sent a shiver down my spine. The last one was of me in a bathroom stall puking my guts out, and I realized with a jolt of pure terror that it was from last night at the club. The caption read *'You'll be on your knees for me soon enough'*.

"How did he get this picture? I was alone in that bathroom!" I insisted, feeling a bubble of hysteria building in my chest. "Alexis, how could you not tell me about this?" My voice cracked. All these months I'd felt like someone was watching me and I'd just brushed it off, but it was true. Someone had been following me, photographing me...The memory of the guy staring at me from the corner of the club resurfaced, and I rubbed my arms to get rid of the goosebumps that had appeared. Was he the guy who'd been in the bathroom with me?

"I didn't want to scare you!" Alexis buried her face in her hands. "I thought it was just another stupid spam account, but every time I would block it another one would spring up. When he started showing up at places where you'd be, that's when I got the police involved. I'm so sorry, I let you down." She burst into tears, and Layla moved over to comfort her. I wasn't at the comforting stage yet. I was still in the stunned and fucking horrified stage. I thought back to last night, wishing my stupid drunken brain could remember any details at all that could be helpful. I couldn't remember hearing anything in the bathroom that night, but my face had been in the toilet, so I'd been a little preoccupied I guess. I closed the file and shoved it back across the table.

"Who is this guy? What does he want with me anyway?" I asked, more to the police sergeant since Alexis was still sobbing into Layla's shoulder. It wasn't exactly fair, I should be the one sobbing right now. I could feel tears prickling the backs of my eyes, but I think the fear had frozen them in place for now. They'd come later, once I was alone again I'm sure.

"We aren't sure yet, I'm afraid. We're having our tech analysts review his accounts and see if we can get some more info from there. The messages he sends are decidedly...mixed." He offered a small smile, his eyes filled with pity. "It's hard to tell at this point what his exact motives are, but we have to assume they aren't innocent."

"Awesome, well...okay, I guess that's good to know then..." What the hell was my next move then? Hide in my condo until some tech nerd tracked an IP to some pervert's mom's basement? Maybe they were going to put me in Witness Protection. I'd have to move to a small town in Ohio and work as a waitress in some diner.

That's for people targeted by the mob you dumbass.

I should probably consider myself lucky the police even gave a shit about this. Actually, that was a good point. Why did the police care about some stalker? He hadn't approached me directly, or done anything to hurt me. Didn't it usually take an actual act of violence for them to even open a file for this kind of thing?

I narrowed my eyes at Sergeant Jeffreys. "Why is this a big deal for you? Do you personally investigate every stalking case that's reported?" With the invention of dating apps and social media, that would mean a metric fuckton of overtime for Sergeant Jeffreys.

The Sergeant cleared his throat, looking uncomfortable. "Well not quite, although I assure you I do not take these things lightly. The young women of our city deserve to be taken seriously. Me Too and all that, you know." Unbelievable. I tried very hard not to roll my eyes at the horrible line of PR nonsense he'd just spouted. I bit my cheek and stayed quiet, waiting for the other shoe to drop.

"Your case is obviously of high priority due to your, uh, celebrity." *Wait for it...* "And obviously your family name holds weight in our community, that can't be overlooked." He admitted, and had the decency to look chagrined. There it was, the real reason I actually mattered to our good ol' boys in blue. Sure, I'd make the news if something happened, my name isn't Kardashian-level by any means, but I still have some standing in my little corner of the internet. But there was no threat quite as motivating as a rich power couple with an axe to grind.

"Yes, of course. My mom would probably feel obligated to sue the department if I end up as some creepy fucker's skin suit." I replied, enjoying seeing the Sergeant squirm. Layla gave me a look of warning, I could feel her begging me to take this seriously. I looked up at the mystery man still lurking in my kitchen, at least he had found my comment amusing. He was stifling a laugh, and I couldn't help but notice the little dimple he had when he smiled.

I had been single for way too long if all it took was a cheek dimple to get me going. I really needed to go on a date, or just get laid, but I guess that was off the table now that some creep was targeting me.

"You mentioned security options?" Layla piped up, her arm still around Alexis. "What can we do?" My heart swelled, and I felt more tears prickle behind my eyes. My wonderful friend, who had probably just wanted to go home and sleep, was once again taking charge of the shit show that was my life. I seriously needed to call someone at the Vatican and check on that sainthood application. Maybe they had a website.

"Right, yes. So I've already discussed with Ms. Masters here, and we both agreed that it would be best if Kacey were to install a security system, and have personal security with her at all times until this problem has been resolved." The Sergeant explained. "Ms. Masters has already taken my advice and hired Everett Cole, who I assure you comes highly recommended. He can even help with the security system, he has connections through his security firm, is that correct?" He looked over at the mystery man, who nodded.

"Personal security? Like a bodyguard?" I asked, giving Mr. Cole a once-over. Of course, he was a bodyguard, the guy was built like a life-sized G.I. Joe action figure. He was missing the sunglasses and the earpiece to really sell it though, but I wasn't sure I could've kept a straight face if he'd shown up looking all Kevin Costner. "Is this maybe, I dunno, a bit much? Sure I can live with a security system. But having hired muscle follow me around feels a bit extreme. No offence." I looked around the table nervously and took another sip of my coffee.

"We would rather be over-prepared than under-prepared in this case I'm afraid." Sergeant Jefferys replied with a sigh. "This stalker has made comments that can be construed as death threats, and he hints towards abduction fantasies in several others. Until we identify him, we cannot be too careful." With that he stood up, making a point of checking his watch. "Now, if you'll excuse me, I'm afraid I must be going. Ms. Masters has my card with my direct line, you can call me with any questions. I will be sure to update you if we find out anything new." He nodded at each of us and Layla showed him out. I would have, but I didn't trust my legs to hold me if I stood up right now.

"Uh, Ms. Keeper? If it's alright with you, I'd like to have a look around your place." Mr. Cole announced, setting his mug down on my counter.

"Call me Kacey, and why exactly?" I asked, immediately defensive. I was definitely not prepared to have a random hot guy wandering around my condo. I thought about the delicates I had hanging to dry and the absolute state my room was in. I'm sure there was a vibrator plugged in somewhere, that would be fun to explain. I guess I could introduce it as my new boyfriend since it's the closest thing I'd have to a real date for a while, it seemed.

"I just need to get the layout of your place, figure out where the cameras should go, what exits we're working with..." He explained, gesturing around as if this wasn't at all surreal. "I'll pick up everything I need today and then I can install it after I get set up. Do you have a spare room I can stay in? Otherwise, I can sleep on the couch just fine."

Jeez, buy a girl a drink first.

Chapter 5

Everett

I'm beginning to think that I have my work cut out for me with this job.

Occasionally, I've had some push-back on the whole personal security thing, and I get it, I would hate it too if I had to pay someone to invade my privacy. I do try to make it as comfortable a process as possible, and despite my size, I do have a knack for fading into the background when I need to.

But the look Kacey gave me when I asked if she had a spare room...it was like I'd asked to take a tour of her underwear drawer. Which I wouldn't be entirely opposed to, if I wasn't on the job that is.

"You're...staying here? For how long?" She asked incredulously. Her hair was dry now, and it fell in dark waves around her face. My fingers itched to tuck one of the loose strands behind her ear. Good grief, what was wrong with me today?

"That all depends on how quickly the police can identify your stalker." I shrugged. "Once the threat is reduced, I can ease up. But for the time being, consider me your shadow." I smiled, hopefully in a reassuring way. Her cheeks coloured, so maybe not as reassuring as I'd hoped.

"Phenomenal. Well, follow me I guess." She sighed and stood, walking out of the kitchen. I trailed after her, taking in the rest of her place. It was big, but not ostentatious. We walked down the hallway, stopping once so she could point out the bathroom, and then once again when we reached her spare room.

"Sorry for the mess, I don't have people stay in here that often," Kacey explained, and then blushed again. "In the spare room, I mean." Something about the way she blushed was oddly alluring. "That couch pulls out into a bed though, I can grab a set of sheets." She wandered over to another door down the hall, presumably a closet, while I looked around. In one corner there was an elliptical machine covered in dust, and across from it was a nice, slightly worn-looking purple couch. A few boxes were stacked up along the walls, some looked old and had handwritten labels like "Keepsakes", while others were clearly newer and had company logos on them. I didn't need much room for my supplies anyway, and most of the tech stuff would be set up in different areas of the house.

"This'll work fine," I told her as she reappeared with a stack of sheets and a pillow. "So where's your room?" She blushed again, and this was going to become a problem for me, I could tell.

"It's down here." She muttered, and I followed her down to the last door at the end of the hallway. She stood at the doorway, clearly uncomfortable, so I tried to be quick. The room was much bigger than the spare bedroom, with a full-sized window and an on-suite bathroom. One side of the room was a lot cleaner than the other, it featured a vanity table with what looked like half of Sephora on top, and a large stand with some kind of hoop at the top that looked like it would light up. The other side of the bed was a disaster, with piles of clothes and empty boxes littering the floor. She had a little mesh drying stand set up in the corner that was covered in panties and bras.

"You aren't putting cameras up in there are you?" She asked as I moved back out into the hall.

"No, the cameras are only for the front entrance, the balcony and the hallway," I assured her. "But I will put sensors on the windows and doors as well just in case."

"We're on the fifth floor. Do you really think this guy is going to Spiderman his way into my bedroom?" Kacey replied, raising an eyebrow at me. I couldn't help but laugh.

"Probably not, but you wouldn't believe the lengths that crazy will go to." I shrugged, shoving my hands in my pockets. Kacey pursed her lips and walked back towards the kitchen where Layla and Alexis were waiting. I pulled out my phone, deciding to give her a little space, and started writing up a list of supplies to send to my tech guy, Jaime. With two exits and only one floor to worry about, the set-up should only take a couple of hours at most. I could have it done tonight if I left soon to grab my gear. Once I sent the list, I headed back into the main area and walked right into an argument.

Chapter 6

Kacey

"You can't be fucking serious right now." I snapped, unable to contain my emotions any longer. I had needles in my brain from the hangover, and an annoying, albeit sexy, thorn in my side named Everett to worry about now. "How am I supposed to work right now, with all of this shit going on?" I waved my arms around, gesturing at the shit that was my life.

"You still have commitments" Alexis insisted, her eyes still red from crying. "We have two new posts to work on that include sponsored materials, and those deadlines are coming up. Contract deadlines." She emphasized, using legalese to trap me once again.

"Fine, whatever, I'll make the stupid videos." I waved impatiently. "But I'm not going out, you can forget about that." That's right, I could just hole up in my condo until everything blew over. You could get anything delivered nowadays, I could stay in here for weeks just fine. Just me, and my new giant roommate Everett apparently.

"Sergeant Jefferys insisted that you should maintain your normal routine," Alexis replied. "If you start acting weird, it could tip him off, or worse. He might escalate his behaviour." She was starting to sound like one of those detectives on the late-night murder shows, and I was annoyed that she was probably right.

"You don't think he'll be tipped off when I show up at a club with some hulking G.I. Joe that's packing heat?" I snapped. Oh great, now I was sounding like some cheesy 80's cop show.

"G.I.'s are army and I was a marine, so technically, I'm a Jarhead," Everett had entered the kitchen again at some point, so silently that I hadn't heard him come up behind me. For a big guy, he was sure quiet. "And I agree with Alexis, you shouldn't deviate from your routine in

23

any way that could give this guy a reason to go to ground. We need to be able to find him."

I grimaced at him, but he ignored it. "If it helps, I don't have to go as your bodyguard. Introduce me as your date, or your brother, whatever works." He smirked at me, the word *date* making my stomach flip. Layla was watching me closely, and I knew she was trying not to laugh. I opened my mouth to give him what would have been an epic and clever retort, but he beat me to the punch.

"I need to stop by my office and pick up a few things. Are you okay to stay here for a bit by yourself? I can give you my cell in case you need you need to reach me." He held out a hand, for my phone presumably. I unlocked it and handed it to him, watching as he typed in his contact info.

"There. I should only be a couple of hours, so unless it's an emergency please stay here until I get back." He flashed me a quick smile, showing off that dimple again, before handing back my phone. I just nodded like an idiot and watched him head to the door. Damn, he had a nice ass too.

Layla barely waited until the door was closed before she practically exploded. "Holy crap, who do I have to piss off to get a security detail like that." She gushed, fanning herself with her hand. I rolled my eyes at her. "If you want him so much, take him. And the super creepy number one fan that comes with him."

"Ugh." Her smile falling. "Right, you're right. I'm sorry hun. This whole thing sucks ass." She gave Alexis a look. "And it's not your fault okay? You did the right thing." Alexis smiled half-heartedly, but she looked tired.

"Layla's right." I agreed, trying my best to relieve some of her guilt. "You know how I obsess over these things, it's why I gave you the job in the first place. I would overreact to every weirdo who commented and probably never leave my bedroom. And I'd never have been brave enough to go to the police, so thank you." I gave her a smile, and it seemed to cheer her up somewhat.

"Now, both of you, get out of here so I can get some sleep. I've got a hot date with a guy and a video camera tonight." I gave Layla a wink, but none of us were really in the mood for jokes. Stalkers do tend to suck the fun out of things.

Alexis was hesitant to leave me by myself, but I convinced her that I needed the peace and quiet to record the new content she needed. After she left, I just needed to convince Layla that just because we had found out about the creep today, didn't mean I would be attacked the second I was alone. She reluctantly gathered her things and headed out, only after insisting I text her every few hours as - *proof of life* - her words, not mine. Once I was alone, the panic finally started to set in. Alexis had left the file on the table, but I wasn't ready to look at that again just yet. After triple-locking the front door, I barricaded myself in my bedroom and tried to get a few hours of sleep.

I tossed and turned for ages before I finally managed to drift off into an equally fitful sleep. By the time I woke, it was late afternoon and the last of my hangover had thankfully faded. I had a quick bite to eat and started working on the content I had promised Alexis, which was a review of some new foundation that boasted minimized pores and an even application. I had already finished testing it, so I just needed to film the video, edit and upload it for Alexis. I got busy setting up my recording space and managed to get about halfway through before the doorbell rang, forcing me to take a break.

Walking to the door, I stood on my tiptoes to peek out the peephole. "Who is it?" I called loudly, trying to sound brave and possibly armed. Maybe I should get a dog, a really big one with a scary bark that I could train to attack guys on command. At least then I'd have someone to talk to around here.

"It's Everett Cole, Miss - Kacey. Can I come in?" Like I had a choice. With a sigh, I let him in, raising my eyebrows at the boxes in his arms.

"What's that, a build-your-own panic room?" I asked, and he huffed a laugh as he set them down on the floor.

"Nothing that exciting I'm afraid. These are just the cameras and the alarm sensors." He replied and then swung the largest backpack I had ever seen off his back, setting it down against the wall. How strong was this guy anyway? He wasn't even breathing heavily after hefting all of that up here. At some point he had taken off his dress shirt he'd been wearing this morning, opting instead for a plain black t-shirt that looked like it was a size too small. It clung to his body, barely stretching over his broad shoulders and showing off his toned physique. He had a sleeve of tattoos wrapping around his left arm from his wrist to up underneath his shirt. When he turned towards me I could see a hint of the tattoo curling up along his neck. It looked like a black flame was licking at his ear. He caught me staring and I looked away quickly, blushing. I was going to get sued for sexual harassment if I kept ogling him like this. The poor guy was just trying to do his job and the lonely spinster he's trying to protect is lusting after him like some creep. Maybe my stalker and I did have something in common after all, ugh.

"I've got some work to finish, are you all good here?" I gestured at the pile of electronics he had obviously been sifting through without my help this whole time. He nodded, his lips quirked up in a hint of a smile. "Okay great, just holler if you need me." I scurried off to my room before I could embarrass myself further, ignoring the butterflies I got when he smiled at me and all but ran to my room.

Alright, back to work. I needed to focus on the deadlines, and not the guy in my living room, or the guy in the bushes snapping pictures of me. Should be easy enough right? Work was normally, well, not exactly fun. But it wasn't usually this hard. Something about the attractive man wandering around my apartment was really throwing off my groove. Not to mention that nagging feeling in my gut that just knew there was a creep out there in the world just waiting for me to post my new video.

I rushed to finish it, and when I finally sent the footage to Alexis, I knew it wasn't my best work. I packed up my laptop and started to clear off my workspace where all the makeup I'd used was spread out. Some of it I'd keep, especially if it was good or if I needed to make more content with it for the sponsors, but if it wasn't my favourite it went into a box for donation. I got so many samples, that the donation boxes filled up pretty quickly.

A knock at the door made me jump, had I actually forgotten that Everett was there? He really was unbelievably quiet for such a big guy. "Ya?" I called out, cringing at myself.

"Sorry, if you don't mind I just need to install the sensors on the windows." He stuck his head in, and when I didn't say no he walked in holding a handful of wires.

"Sure, not a problem," I replied breezily and finished packing up the rest of my things. I watched him out of the corner of my eye as he started attaching one of the cables around the top of my bedroom window. His shirt rode up his back as he stretched his arms up to reach the top of the window sill, and I stared at the patch of skin wistfully.

I had been single for way too long if that was enough to get me all hot and bothered. He finished up and I quickly turned back to my set-up so he didn't catch me leering at him. I turned off my ring light and stowed it back in the corner so I wouldn't trip over it in the night. "What is that thing anyway?" Everett asked, pointing at it.

"This? It's a ring light. It gives me even light for my videos so there are no weird shadows on my face." I explained, but this didn't seem like the answer he was looking for, because he still looked confused. "All done in here?" I continued, looking at the little black box he'd attached to the side of my window.

"Almost." He smiled, "I just have to do the bathroom window and then you're all set." He walked past me, his arm just brushing mine. I could feel the warmth coming off of him, and a blush crept up my face.

He walked out of the bathroom a minute later. "Oh...uh...sorry. I just need to move this..." Everett held up - to my absolute horror - my purple vibrator. I'd plugged it into the outlet in my bathroom and set it on the window sill to charge.

"I'll take that thanks!" I yelped, snatching it away. Where was a lightning bolt when I needed one? One eyebrow quirked, Everett at least had the decency not to laugh in my face. He stepped back into the bathroom as I moved to the nearby dresser and shoved the vibrator in behind my clothes.

I hoped they found my stalker soon before I actually dropped dead of embarrassment.

Chapter 7

Everett

After the rather unusual incident in the bathroom, I got out of Kacey's room as quickly as I could and hunkered down for the night in the spare room. The security system was all set up, and after a quick test and a couple of updates, it was up and running. I flipped through the cameras one at a time, checking the angles to make sure there weren't any glaring blind spots I'd need to worry about. I really wasn't expecting anyone to climb up five stories and try to break in through the balcony, but it wasn't completely out of the question. The stalker had proved he was stealthy enough to get close to Kacey without detection, so maybe he would be desperate enough to buy some climbing gear in order to bypass the security guard at the front door.

When I went to check the hallway camera, I caught Kacey tiptoeing toward the kitchen, obviously trying to avoid me. I waited a few minutes to make sure she wasn't trying to sneak out of the condo without me, and then she reappeared, carrying a pint of ice cream and a spoon back to her room. I smiled and listened for her door to shut, then finished checking the rest of the cameras. I switched on the alarm from my phone, so if any windows or doors opened I would be alerted immediately, even if we weren't home at the time.

With that complete, I checked my phone for any new notifications. Jaime had set up some kind of notification system that would alert me if Kacey or her stalker posted anything new. He had also set me up with my very own fake account so I could look through their accounts and view any of their old posts. I'd gone over the stalker's posts more than once, mainly looking for patterns or any clues to his identity, but nothing had come up so far. Not ready to sleep just yet, I decided to look through Kacey's. Maybe this would help me finally understand what the hell she actually did for this job of hers.

I scrolled through her photos, but they didn't answer my questions. She looked amazing in all of them, but it felt fake somehow. These pictures didn't seem to connect with the person I'd been talking to today, the woman who got hungover and walked around naked and left vibrators on the windowsill. I smirked at the memory. If she wasn't a client, I would have offered to show her some fun ways to use that vibrator. Something about the way Kacey blushed made my dick hard. Giving up on the picture feed, I switched over to her channel, Kacey's Keepers, where she posted her longer videos. These seemed a bit more interesting.

I watched a few of the newer videos, and they seemed very...professional. They felt fake like the pictures, she was smiling in them, but it wasn't a genuine smile, never quite reaching her eyes. I scrolled back to some of the first videos she'd made. These ones were clearly done without all the fancy gear, and Kacey looked quite a bit younger. I checked the date on one of them, and it had been posted nearly 10 years ago. Now this video showed an authentic version of Kacey. Here she was a bubbly young adult, cracking jokes and showing how to apply mascara. The end of the video showed her jumping into a pool fully clothed, announcing that the water-proof mascara was, in fact, a 'Keeper'. This was entertaining, and fit more with the woman I'd met today. I closed my laptop and stared up at the ceiling of the little spare room. Is that what fame does to a person? Did it really have the power to turn them into a watered-down shadow of their former selves? Or had something happened that had caused that? Comparing it to some of the newer posts I'd seen, it looked as if her spark had gone out, and she no longer seemed to enjoy what she was doing.

Putting that thought aside for the night, I set my alarm for 7:00 a.m. and went over the schedule for tomorrow one more time. At everyone's insistence, Kacey had agreed to stick to her normal routine. Tomorrow was Sunday, so she had hot yoga - whatever the fuck *that* was - at 8:30 a.m., and then a launch party for a new makeup line at

4:00 p.m. Kacey had insisted that I be as inconspicuous as possible, so I'd asked for Alexis to book me in the class as well. Nothing would stick out more than some random guy standing in the corner watching a yoga class.

I'd brought some nicer clothes, including a suit jacket, that I could wear to the launch party. Apparently, the party was not black-tie, but cocktail formal? Fuck if I knew what that meant, but usually men had an easier time with dress codes anyway. I figured a suit would be enough, and I would love to see someone try to call me out on it if it wasn't. As long as we weren't going to too many fancy events I should be fine for at least a week with what I'd brought with me. Depending on how long this job went, I might have to make a stop back home or ask Kacey where the laundry room was.

I set my phone down and closed my eyes, willing my body to relax in this unfamiliar room. This wasn't even close to the hardest job I've ever done, or the worst accommodations I'd had. I hadn't been joking when I offered to sleep on her couch, it beat sleeping on the floor at least. And going with Kacey to some workout classes and a few cocktail parties? I was once in a helicopter that got shot out of the sky, this was almost a vacation by comparison. There was no way yoga could be worse than crash-landing in the desert under heavy gunfire...right?

Chapter 8

Everett

"You cannot seriously tell me that people do this for fun." I gasped, collapsing onto my stomach. The drill sergeant - sorry, yogi - hit the gong at the front of the room, finally signalling the end of the class. It had to be at least a hundred degrees in this room, and there was a literal puddle of sweat soaking into my yoga mat underneath me. My arms and legs felt like jello, and at one point I think I might've passed out for a few minutes. I've been working out for years, but I've never come as close to crying as I did after the sixth round of sun salutations. It should be illegal for them to ask us for money after forcing us to exercise in a damn sauna.

Kacey was sitting on the mat beside me, laughing at my pain. She was breathing hard after the workout, her chest rising and falling under her blue sports bra. I thought she'd been joking about the heat when we got here, and I figured I would be fine in my muscle shirt and gym shorts. Not even ten minutes into the class the muscle shirt had come off, tossed into a soggy heap in the corner. I should've realized something was fishy when everyone seemed to have a towel with them when there was clearly no pool in sight. Still lying on my stomach, I watched Kacey take a few swigs of water, small beads of sweat running down between her breasts. Fuck, well there was at least one muscle in my body that was still up for a workout. I focused on the pain in my arms instead, hoping I could stand up without Kacey noticing my excitement. I definitely needed a cold shower as soon as possible.

"Do I need to call someone? A paramedic?" Kacey teased, finally standing up. She grabbed a spray bottle and a rag off the nearby table and sprayed her mat, I guess to clean off the sweat and tears to get it ready for the next person.

"No," I grunted, pushing myself onto all fours, and then carefully up to stand. "But I think you need a shrink. Who pays money to get tortured like that?" I took the spray bottle from her, imitating her steps to clean and stow the mat. I probably should have rung mine out first like a sponge, but this would have to do.

I grabbed my shirt from the corner, it was still damp but that was okay, I only had to wear it until we got back to the condo. Kacey had warned me before the class that we'd need to shower afterwards, and boy was she right.

I waited for her to gather up her things and then we headed out of the torture chamber and into the blissfully cool morning air. When we arrived, Kacey had pointed out a nice little coffee shop nearby, and she decided that we should stop for breakfast before heading home. Still wearing just her sports bra and leggings, Kacey strode confidently into the cafe with me close behind. I guess they must get a lot of sweaty yoga students as customers because no one batted an eye at our appearances.

Kacey ordered herself an iced coffee and some kind of croissant-sandwich hybrid, while I ordered the largest coffee they could give me and three sandwiches, not even bothering to find out what was in them. I had already finished the first two by the time the third one was brought out, Kacey watching me wide-eyed as she finished her own sandwich. Normally I tried to have a bit more manners when I was out with a woman, but I was nearly feral with hunger after that brutal class.

"So you've really never done yoga before?" Kacey asked once I came up for air. I shook my head and took a sip of my coffee.

"I've done plenty of stretching before, but nothing that intense," I explained. "Why do they make it so hot?" I was still sweating, and I probably should've gotten water instead of coffee to try and rehydrate.

"They say it's good for your muscles, but it really just makes you sweat a ton." Kacey shrugged, sipping her drink. "People can lose like 5 lbs in one class just from sweating so much."

"That sounds horrible." I laughed. "How do you actually enjoy it?"

"I don't enjoy it, but that's not the point." Kacey laughed. "Think of it like...Sunday confession for Catholics. I sweat out my sins to get ready for the week ahead." She winked and stood up, grabbing her coffee. "Let's get home, I need a shower." She announced.

There were other ways to sweat out your sins that were much more fun than hot yoga, but I kept that little comment to myself. I grabbed my coffee and brought our plates to the counter, then followed her out to my car. I'd driven us here since it turned out Kacey didn't actually have her own vehicle at the moment. Not that I blamed her, if you lived downtown everything was either within walking distance or a 5-minute cab ride.

"Question for you." Kacey mused as I opened the passenger side door for her, since she refused to sit in the back while I drove. "I thought bodyguards were supposed to have, like, weapons. You know, in case we get attacked or something?" I laughed as I slid into my seat and started the car.

"What makes you think I don't?" I asked her, and Kacey looked me up and down, one eyebrow raised. "You're in gym shorts, where you could possibly have a weapon?"

"You'd be surprised." I shot her a wicked grin while pulling out of the parking spot. Heat coloured her cheeks and my dick gave a little jump. I needed to get that under control before I got fired.

"To answer your question, I do normally carry a gun when I'm on the job," I explained. "And I normally have a knife or two as well. For situations like this, I'll stow a knife in my shoe so it's nearby, but my go-to would be to neutralize the threat with something nearby or just my fists in my pinch. This is a pretty rare case though, I'm normally dressed when I'm working." I smiled, and she laughed. Kacey seemed to be warming up to me a bit, which made the job easier. The best I can hope for is that the client is comfortable and trusts me with their safety. If I can make them laugh? Well, that's just a bonus I guess.

Chapter 9

Kacey

"Goddamn fuck! Fuck this fucking dress!" I snarled, fighting the stubborn piece of fabric that was currently making my life a living hell. I added it to the list, just above 'hot guy living in my house that I couldn't touch' but underneath 'Creepy stalker'. That one would be hard to top at this point.

My hair was passable, my makeup was done, and we were still going to be late to the launch party all because the fucking zipper of my dress had decided to get stuck between my shoulder blades, right where I couldn't reach it. My arms were already so tired from yoga this morning that they refused to stretch the extra millimetre I needed to grab it.

Yoga had at least been invigorating, in more ways than one. At first, I'd been mortified that Everett had decided to join, rather than skulk outside the studio like I'd assumed he would. It was quite a sight to see him reduced to a sweaty disaster, clearly having never attended a hot yoga class before. I did try to warn him...sort of. I'm not sure anyone in the class had been able to concentrate on their poses after he took off his shirt though. His tattoo was much bigger than it had first appeared, stretching across his shoulder and down along one shoulder blade. His abs were...wow. I had never seen muscles like that outside of an action movie. I couldn't stop staring at his arms and the way the muscles looked as they strained in plank pose. I could almost imagine how it would feel if they picked me up and pinned me to the wall, what it would be like to trace my hand along the lines of his tattoo...

Good grief, I really needed to stop lusting after the man who was just trying to do his job. I tried my best to take care of things myself in the shower, but all I could think about was how my vibrator couldn't compare to what Everett was packing under those gym shorts.

So now here I was, sore, horny, and trapped in a godforsaken dress for an event I didn't even want to go to in the first place. I grabbed my purse, still only half in my dress, and walked out into the kitchen where Everett was waiting. Damn it, of course, he looked amazing in a suit too. He had a dark red dress shirt on, but the collar was unbuttoned and relaxed. He'd showered too obviously, and his short black hair was carefully styled instead of its regular tousled look. He looked up when I walked in, and I felt his gaze rake over me, making me blush again. I really needed to wear more foundation if my face was going to be this red all the time.

"You've got hands." I pointed out, like he hadn't noticed before today. "Would you mind helping me with my zipper?" I turned to show him the problem.

"Sure thing." He pushed off the counter and cleared the space between us in a heartbeat. Ever so gently, he lifted my hair off my back and let it fall over my shoulder so it was out of the way. I tried not to shiver when his fingers brushed lightly against my back, tracing down my spine until they reached the zipper. I could feel his breath on my neck as he pressed close, working the zipper carefully so as not to rip the dress. Finally, it popped free and the zipper pulled up. I let out a breath I didn't know I'd been holding and quickly stepped away from the warmth of his body.

"Perfect, thanks!" I managed to squeak. "Let's get this over with, shall we?" He laughed and I let him open the door for me since he seemed to like to do that. I wasn't sure if that was a bodyguard thing or just him being a gentleman, but either way, it was unexpectedly sweet.

The ride to the venue was a silent affair, Everett was concentrating on the directions his GPS was shouting at him, and I was busy rethinking my life choices. Why had I agreed to go to this event? It would just be a bunch of strangers wanting to talk to me and take pictures with me. What if one of them was him? I wouldn't even know who to look for. This guy was just a faceless shadow who'd decided to haunt me. And why? Why me? What had I done to make him think I wanted this kind of attention?

No, fuck that. I didn't do anything, this was all on him.

Everett pulled into the hotel parking lot, following the signs for the private function being hosted today. From there it was easy enough to just follow the similarly dressed groups of people who were making their way into the main lobby. He was sweet enough to offer his arm, and I accepted - partially for the chance to touch him without being weird about it - but mostly because I was wearing heels and the uneven pavement was a tripping hazard. Bolstered by his steadiness, I plastered on my fake smile and got myself into a networking headspace.

Once we entered the main function room, noise exploded around us. Circling the room were beautiful displays of the new make-up line being launched. Everyone with at least half a million followers was being encouraged to try on different items and sample bags were being handed out left and right. Along one side of the room was the bar, and servers were circulating with trays of tiny appetizers and champagne. Everett declined a glass, because drinking on the job was frowned upon. In my line of work, however, it was fairly encouraged. I took a glass, needing the liquid courage and something to do with my hands. I finished it more quickly than I probably should have, and like magic, it was replaced by another full glass - that could be very dangerous. Sipping this glass more slowly, I stepped off to the side with Everett so I could take in the room and quickly work out my plan of attack.

"I'm going to head over to that table over there," I told him, pointing over to the left of the room, where a lovely woman in a Chanel dress was modelling lipsticks. "You can hang back by the bar if you want, I won't be long." I looked behind us, and sure enough, it looked like every male 'plus one' at the event had been given the same instructions. The front of the bar had turned into a veritable Abercombie and Fitch reunion. Everett hesitated for a moment, but even he knew it would've looked odd if he was glued to my side the entire time, so he meandered over to the bar and leaned against it, trying to blend in.

I finished my champagne and set the empty glass on a nearby table before heading over to the lipstick display. They were nice, I had to admit. The new line was promoting a lipstick that boasted no smearing or flaking, and the range of colours was expansive. I did a few swatches, mimicking the other women around me, and got some casual pictures that Alexis could use in my stories. At my request, one of the women managing the display grabbed me a couple of samplers in different shades, and then helped me apply the one she insisted would be the best suited for my face.

Looking in the mirror, she definitely wasn't wrong. It was a strong red, with hints of orange, and it was truly striking with my somewhat pasty complexion. Definitely bolder than my everyday style, but it was fun to get outside my comfort zone now and then.

"Hey there." An unfamiliar hand slid around my waist, and my blood turned to ice. I stepped away, spinning around aggressively, and just narrowly avoided colliding with a woman trying to get a selfie with the Chanel girl.

"Whoa, what the hell Kace? I don't have cooties, Jesus." The blood rushed back into my limbs as I realized who that smug, whiney voice belonged to.

"Oh, Rex." I sighed. Of course, he would be here. He was also a model-turned-influencer and he'd done a lot of work for this brand in the past. Clearly not deterred by initial reaction, he took another step closer, until I could smell the whiskey on his breath.

"Did you get that picture I sent the other night?" He sneered, and I tried not to gag.

Some day I would invent a time machine, go back in time and slap myself for ever hooking up with this sentient poop emoji. "Sorry, I didn't." I shrugged, taking another step back and grabbing a glass of champagne from a passing server. "I got a new phone. Anyway, I should go mingle, bye!" I pushed into the crowd before he could respond, losing myself in a crowd of estrogen and eyeshadow. I swear he'd had at least one redeemable quality when I'd agreed to go out with him, but I couldn't remember what it had been. Maybe I'd just been really lonely that night.

I lost track of how long I stood around chatting and posing with everyone at the event, trapped in the endless cycle of greetings and small talk. My feet were aching and my cheeks were starting to hurt from all the smiling. The third glass of champagne was long gone and starting to go to my head. It seemed like everyone felt the need to touch me in some way, either with a hand on my shoulder or around my waist. Women I had never met before kissed me on the cheek, and men would grab my elbow while they talked to pull me closer to them. All the while I felt that prickle on the back of my neck, wondering and dreading if my stalker was somewhere in this room, watching me. What if he was one of the people nearby, so close he could even reach out and grab me if he wanted?

My chest was starting to constrict, and I suddenly felt the overwhelming desire to be anywhere but in this room. Weaving my way around the booths and the people around them, I spotted a side door along the far wall and bee-lined towards it, shoving it open and stumbling into the empty hallway. I closed my eyes and embraced the silence, leaning against the wall while I tried to catch my breath. It felt like I couldn't get air in my lungs, no matter how hard I tried.

I heard the door open again, and then someone was standing very, very close to me. "Kacey, what's wrong? I turned for a second and you had disappeared!" I opened my eyes to find Everett staring down at me, looking concerned.

"I couldn't...I can't...breathe..." I gasped, rubbing my chest with my hand as if that could remove the invisible boulder that was slowly crushing me.

Chapter 10

Everett

I'd managed to keep track of Kacey for over an hour as she moved through the crowds of people, but it hadn't been easy. While I was keeping an eye on her, I was also trying to spot anyone else who seemed to be overly interested in her. For the moment at least, aside from the odd person who came up to her to chat directly, it didn't seem like anyone besides me was watching her. I held a glass of whiskey, untouched, to sell the act that I was just a date waiting for my girl by the bar. Every few minutes I'd bring it up to my lips without actually drinking any. I was already thinking some pretty dirty thoughts about my client, I shouldn't add alcohol to that mix.

Kacey sure wasn't making it easy for me to stay professional. When she had come out wearing that slinky green dress I'd nearly lost my cool. It had taken all the willpower I had to zip it up and not just rip it the rest of the way off and show her all the ways I could make her blush.

Just then, someone jostled me, knocking my arm enough to dump my decoy drink all over myself and the floor. "Watch where you're going." I snapped, but they were already gone, and without even a sorry. "Asshole," I muttered and grabbed some cocktail napkins off the bar to dab up what I could off my jacket. It was only a moment's distraction, but it was enough. By the time I looked back into the crowd, I'd lost Kacey.

"Son of a bitch." I muttered, scanning around where she'd just been standing, but it was as if she'd melted into the floor. I started walking towards that side of the room, trying to look as casual as possible. I was about to give up and call her cell when I saw someone with dark hair and a green dress dart through one of the service doors behind the booths. Stepping up my pace, I skirted around behind the booths to bypass the crowds and slipped out through the same door. The door led to a back hallway that must have been used by the hotel staff to transport food and event decorations to and from the venue hall. I spotted Kacey leaning up against the nearby wall, her eyes closed and face twisted in panic.

Relief flooded through me when I saw her, safe and - well, sound might've been a bit of a stretch, but in one piece at least. I was at her side in a heartbeat, trying to figure out what had happened in two minutes that had caused this...whatever it was. She didn't look physically hurt, that much I could tell. But something was obviously causing her distress.

"I can't breathe." Kacey gasped out, looking up at me with panic in her eyes. Without thinking, I grabbed her hand and put it flat against my chest. "Here, just breathe like me, okay?" I instructed gently. Taking a big breath in, I held it for a moment, then let it out slowly. I kept her hand pressed against my chest, letting her feel it rise and fall with my breath.

"I didn't know that make-up could be so terrifying" I teased, trying to lighten the mood and ease her panic. She shuddered a small laugh, and her breathing slowed down, gradually returning to normal.

"See? You're okay, it was just a little panic attack." I told her. "You're going to be fine." I watched her chest rise and fall as she took a few more steady, slow breaths.

She was looking up at me, her green eyes sparkling and her cheeks flushed. I was acutely aware of how close I was to her, nearly pressing her into the wall. Her soft hand was still in mine, pressing up against my chest. I should drop her hand since she no longer needed my help to breathe, but I kept holding it, not quite willing to let her go.

"Everett..." She murmured, her eyes drifting down to my lips. Her own parted ever so slightly as if inviting me in. A fierce hunger rose up in me, desperate to taste her. I had to reign this in quickly before I did something we'd both regret.

I let go of her hand, dropping mine back to my side. "Would you like to go back inside for a bit longer, or should I maybe take you home?" I asked, trying to diffuse the moment before it got out of hand.

Evidently, Kacey had other ideas. Instead of pulling her hand away from my chest, she grabbed a fistful of my shirt and yanked me closer. For someone so small, she was surprisingly strong - probably all of that hot yoga. Before I could say another word, she wrapped her other hand around the back of my neck, pulling me down low enough so that she could press her lips onto mine.

So, that's what they meant by a kiss so good you saw fireworks. Her lips sent white hot fire through my body, and whatever self-control I had left was completely burned away. I grabbed the side of her face, tracing along her jaw and tilting her chin up for a better angle. I kissed her back hungrily, pressing my body flush with hers until she was completely pinned against the wall. Kacey let out a little gasp, and I used that to part her lips further with my tongue, exploring every inch of her mouth. That move earned me a soft moan, and her hips rocked against me, pressing against my already hard cock. My hand slid down her side to grab her hips, pulling her up higher so she could feel just how badly I wanted her. I moved my mouth down to press kisses along her jaw, then down her neck, pausing to nibble and suck on her earlobe.

"Oh fuck, Everett" Kacey moaned, one hand still gripping my shirt and the other now fisted in my hair. She hitched up her leg, wrapping it around my hip, grinding against my cock. God damn it she was so hot, I could hardly stand it. I moved back to her mouth, kissing her furiously and tasting the champagne on her tongue. My hand slid up her thigh, pushing her dress up higher. It was so tempting, the thought of fucking her in this hallway, not even caring who might walk in at any moment.

Some small part of my brain that was still somehow receiving blood flow sent up a warning flare. I tensed slightly, and sure enough, I heard footsteps echoing down the hallway. I quickly pulled back from Kacey, reaching behind my back for the gun I had hidden under my jacket.

Whoever it was had vanished, but I'm sure I saw the outline of a person disappearing around the corner.

"What's wrong? Who was that?" Kacey asked quietly. I shifted my jacket back into place, turning to look at her. Her lips were swollen and parted, and she looked a little breathless, but in a good way this time. Her dress was still hiked up her thigh, and I felt a pang of disappointment as she pulled it down, smoothing it back into place.

"Nothing...it's fine." I murmured, not wanting to scare her unnecessarily. The moment was ruined though, both of us sobering up to the reality of our situation. "We should probably get going." She nodded, fumbling with her purse and pulling out a compact mirror.

"Well I'll be damned, that really is a smear-proof lipstick." She smiled.

Chapter 11
Kacey

It was evening by the time we got back to the condo, so I ordered some takeout from a nearby Thai place. Everett volunteered to meet the delivery guy in the lobby, probably looking for any excuse to get away from his sex-crazed employer. What had I been thinking, dry-humping him in a hallway like we were in high school? He just made me feel so safe, talking me down from the panic that had been threatening to crush me. I wanted to stay wrapped in those arms - to know what he would've done to me if we hadn't been interrupted...

Good grief, I was like a cat in heat.

While Everett was out, I changed out of my dress - of course, the zipper came *off* no problem - and put on a simple pair of leggings and a tank top. I was just setting some plates and cutlery out when he returned bearing an armful of food.

"How much did you order exactly?" He asked me, setting the bags down on the table.

"A lot." I smiled. "I like having leftovers, saves me from cooking tomorrow." He smiled and helped me set out the containers, then helped himself at my insistence. We had just settled into a comfortable silence when his phone went off. He put down his fork to check it, apparently not much of a multi-tasker, and I continued to eat, more than used to my dining partners having their phones at the table. After a few minutes, I noticed that a little crease had appeared between his eyebrows, his food long forgotten.

"Hey, everyone okay in there?" I asked, hopeful that it was somehow completely unrelated to me. He looked up and I could tell that I wasn't going to be so lucky. He slid his phone across the table, and my stomach turned to lead. There on his screen was a picture of me with my tongue down Everett's throat, the caption below it read *YOU CHEATING BITCH.*

"Oh my god. Oh shit. Oh *shit!*" I stood up, backing away from the phone like it was a live snake. "He was there. He was right there, how did I not see him? Oh god. This is totally fucked up." I was definitely spiralling. Not only was this guy apparently a ghost, he was now a very pissed-off ghost. I'd been careless and stupid and now my make-out session with Everett was all over the internet.

"Oh crap, you won't get fired for this will you? Please tell me I didn't just get you fired." I was so stupid. So so stupid. I went over to my fridge and grabbed a bottle of white wine I'd opened a couple of days ago. I poured myself a glass and then downed it, grimacing at the slightly sour tinge it had. *Come on Kacey, use your brain for once.*

"Maybe I can call your boss, I'll explain that it was my fault, I basically attacked your face, and you shouldn't be reprimanded for it." I poured a second glass, continuing my pacing as my mind raced. "You can't be fired if I sexually harassed you right? Oh fuck, would they sue me for that?" I was moving to a convent in Europe first thing in the morning. No men, no stalkers, and maybe I could finally make some progress on that sainthood application for Layla.

Everett had gotten up and was standing in front of me, blocking my path. He grabbed my arms gently to stop me, but this train of thought had already left the station. "I'm really sorry about all of this. If you want to quit that's totally fine, I would understand. I wasn't thinking when I kissed you, it was all just a big mistake -" I stopped with a squeak as he lifted me off my feet like it was nothing and set me down on the kitchen counter. What, was he putting me in a timeout or something?

"Listen," Everett told me, looking me in the eyes. "This is not your fault. Someone took your picture without your permission, and my guy is already working on getting it taken down." He explained, gently taking the glass out of my hand and setting it down beside me. "As for getting me fired, that's not likely to happen, seeing how it's my company." He smiled, showing off that dimple again. He was infuriatingly calm about everything, it would drive me crazy if he wasn't so damn hot.

"What?" I said dumbly. "I thought you just worked for L.T.C. Security?" He was standing very close to me again, trapping me on the counter.

"I'm the owner and operator. My team and I work as independent contractors for bigger companies, and then we get other jobs through the contacts I've made." He was smiling at me, his fingers brushing lightly against my thigh. Without thinking, my legs drifted apart, leaving him room to shift up between my thighs.

"What does L.T.C. stand for?" I asked, my breath hitching as his fingers traced little circles higher up my thigh. My core was aching, and I could feel my panties getting damp as the space between us grew smaller.

"Lieutenant Cole." He chuckled sheepishly. "It's not the most original, I know. My sister came up with it." His other hand had moved up to tease the bottom of my tank top.

We were getting tantalizingly close to where we'd left off back in the hallway, and in the back of my mind, I knew I should put a stop to it. It would be opening a can of worms if I started fooling around with the guy being paid to stay in my condo. But for some reason, I couldn't bring myself to stop his hands, and my own reached up of their own accord, wrapping around his neck. I had so much pent-up stress from the last couple of days, and I was desperate for the release that Everett was offering, consequences be damned.

"If it makes you feel better, we could still go through the official channels for this," Everett murmured, his fingers slipping up under my shirt and brushing lightly against my spine. My back arched when he hit a ticklish spot, and my breasts pressed against his firm chest. I could feel my nipples start to harden against him. His other hand was still tracing light circles on my leg, but it was moving ever so slowly up along my inner thigh, teasingly close to my aching pussy.

"You would need to submit a complaint to HR," Everett whispered, his lips brushing against my ear. "But, since I'm head of the HR department, I would insist that you write down in extreme detail exactly what it is that I did to you, and how it made you feel." His fingers shifted between us, pressing firmly against my clit. I moaned loudly, and the hand on my back pulled me even tighter against him, so there was no way I could escape the pressure from his thumb. I tangled a hand in his hair, gripping him roughly as my eyes shuttered closed.

"Fuck, you are so sexy." He groaned, moving his thumb in slow, agonizing circles around my clit. I clenched my thighs and hooked my legs around him in case he got any dumb ideas about walking away. With a chuckle, he increased the speed of his circles until I was trembling under his hand.

"Everett..." I whimpered, thrusting desperately against his hand. I could already an aching pressure building up in my core. I wanted him, no I *needed* him.

"You're so wet Kace." He breathed, brushing his lips against my neck. "Let go for me baby, I want to see you come apart." I threw my head back as the building pressure finally crested and I climaxed hard, my legs clenching tightly as wave after wave of pleasure rocked through my core. He didn't let up just yet, continuing to stroke and tease me until I was a shuddering mess in his arms. He finally eased his hand off my clit, and I watched as he lifted his hand to his mouth and licked his thumb with a smirk. Why was that so hot?

"You should try to get some sleep." He murmured, pressing a soft kiss to my lips that was over all too quickly and left me hungry for more. He finally stepped away from the counter, freeing me to hop down. My legs were weak, and the look he gave me was so full of lust that I almost said no, just so we could go for round two. Unfortunately, the day was finally starting to catch up with me, and I felt a heaviness in my limbs that I couldn't ignore any longer.

"Goodnight then," I whispered, suddenly feeling a bit self-conscious at how vulnerable I'd been with him. I left him in the kitchen and heard him starting to clear away our forgotten dinner. Everett had given me exactly what my body needed, and that night I was able to fall asleep almost as soon as my head hit the pillow.

Chapter 12

Everett

"Why wasn't this on the schedule Alexis gave me?" I asked, my eyes scanning for an open parking space.

"Because this isn't for work, this is just something I do in my spare time," Kacey replied. She was dressed much more casually today, just jeans and a faded blue tee-shirt, but somehow it was just as sexy as the green dress. Her hair was up in a messy bun today, more function than fashion I gathered, and it showed off her graceful neck. I couldn't stop thinking about how she'd sounded as she came apart in my hand, and that had been with only one finger. Just wait until she found out what I could do with other parts of my body. I shifted in my seat, pulling my attention back to the road. I'd been so hard after she went to bed last night, it had taken every ounce of my self-control to let her walk out of that kitchen. I'd found a little relief with my hand, jerking off in the spare room while thinking about all the things I'd like to do to her, how nice her lips would look around my cock-

Okay, it was this type of thinking that was going to get me into serious trouble. I needed to focus and I needed to be professional. This morning I had managed to keep my hands off of Kacey, which I considered a small triumph. We'd enjoyed a quiet cup of coffee together at the kitchen table. Kacey read her book, I messed around on my phone, and no one mentioned the orgasm on the counter from the night before. She was beautiful first thing in the morning, her hair a messy dark mane around her face. She had still been in her pyjamas, and I could make out the outline of her nipples under her tank top. I was going to need to start taking a cold shower every morning if I was going to make it through this week.

"Oh, there's one!" Kacey announced, pointing out a recently vacated spot just ahead of us. I swung the car into the spot, wishing

it was just a little closer to the entrance. The surrounding area was partially obscured by some hedges, so I wouldn't be able to see if anyone was nearby when we returned.

I was trying not to freak Kacey out, but that picture last night still had me on edge. He had been so close to us and I hadn't heard him, too focused on Kacey to notice anything around us. I clenched the steering wheel briefly, furious that I had been bested by some creep. Kacey - oblivious to my dark mood - hopped out of the car, and I hurried out after her. She refused to wait and let me open the car door for her, saying that it made her feel like a child. She grabbed one of the boxes she had loaded into the trunk, and I grabbed the other two. These were just a few of the many boxes she had stacked up in the spare room, and after being scolded for shaking one - out of sheer curiosity - I had stopped trying to guess what was inside.

Kacey led me, not to the main entrance as I'd expected, but instead to a little side door of a smaller building attached to the hospital. Together we carried the boxes up to the second floor, where she greeted the nurse at the desk with a genuine smile.

"Kat my dear, how have you been?" The older woman smiled back, standing up and coming around the desk to give her a hug. Kacey shifted the box to her hip and gave her a one-armed hug in return. There were hand-drawn pictures and children's crafts hung up along the walls of this wing, and I could hear a cartoon intro song playing from one of the rooms further down the hall. Clearly, this was a children's wing, even the nurses working were wearing colourful scrubs, and their clipboards and carts were decorated with more drawings. Now I was even more curious about what could possibly be in the boxes we were holding.

"Great as always Beth," Kacey told her, earning another squeeze from the nurse. "How are the kiddos today?"

"Excited as usual." Beth smiled. "They're waiting for you in the sunroom." Kacey gestured for me to follow and she and Beth started off down the hall towards the sunroom. Beth glanced at me over her shoulder and gave me an appraising look before turning back to Kacey. "And who is the handsome young man trailing behind you like a lost puppy?" She asked, loudly enough for me to hear.

"That's Everett, he's my...friend," Kacey replied, and I saw that lovely pink flush start creeping up her face before she turned away.

"Mmhmm, I wish I had friends that looked like him." Beth mused, glancing over at me once more. I smiled at her and winked, making her chuckle as she turned back to Kacey.

The sunroom was all the way at the end of the long hallway, and it was aptly named thanks to the wall-to-wall windows along the one side. It reminded me a bit of Kacey's apartment, with all its natural light and the view of the city. That's where the comparisons ended though. This room had a lot more tables, which were scattered around haphazardly, each holding mirrors of different shapes and sizes. There were also a couple of hospital beds lining the wall. Kids, ranging in age from 10 to maybe 17 were milling around. Some were sitting in the chairs around the tables, while others were in wheelchairs. Some of the kids were hooked up to IVs or had oxygen tanks beside them, and the kids in the beds had both. One thing everyone had in common was the look of pure joy that appeared on their faces the moment they saw Kacey enter the room.

"Who's ready to test some makeup!" Kacey exclaimed, and a chorus of cheers went through the room. Everyone here was definitely a fan of Kacey and her channel, and it was heartwarming to watch as the kids swarmed her, asking for hugs and selfies.

As soon as I set the boxes down on one of the tables, the kids converged on them, and I barely made it out of the way with all my limbs still intact. Kacey saw about distributing everything equally, and soon every kid had a small pile of bottles and brushes as well as a mirror in front of them. She walked around to all the tables, offering advice and demonstrating different techniques for applying certain products.

Some of the kids had a harder time than others, and Kacey made sure to spend extra time with them, helping to hold the brush or apply eye shadow in slow, even strokes.

I stayed out of the way, watching for the most part. I tried to lend a hand where I could, like if they needed a new box of tissues or help unscrewing a lid off one of the bottles. Beth appeared periodically with water for Kacey and a cup of coffee for me, which I greatly appreciated. I could tell she held a lot of affection for Kacey, and they'd obviously known each other for quite some time.

"Does she do this kind of thing a lot with the kids?" I asked Beth finally. Kacey seemed at ease here, and there was no trace of that fake smile she put on in her makeup videos. This was the authentic Kacey, just goofing around with makeup and making people happy. It made me happy too, just seeing her light up the room with her smile.

"She comes around every couple of months at least." Beth smiled. "Ever since she was 19. She used to just bring a few things she'd buy with her own money and do makeovers for the kids, but ever since her channel took off she gets all this free stuff, which she claims she has no use for. We'd never be able to afford all this for the kids otherwise." Beth watched fondly as Kacey showed one of the older kids how to apply a thin line of eyeliner so that it flared up at the end.

"Wow, that's pretty incredible," I murmured, watching Kacey dash away to help another kid who was having trouble with some blush.

"It truly is. I can't think of a better way for her to honour her sister." Beth replied, her eyes shining. "Oh now look at me getting all misty." She tutted me like it was my fault. "You are trouble, young man." Giving my arm a playful swat, she headed off back to her desk, chuckling to herself.

Kacey had a sister? I frowned slightly, watching as she laughed and showed one of the older teens how to fill in her eyebrows. She was wearing a pink wool cap, and I could tell she'd been through at least one round of chemo. She'd never mentioned anything about a sister, and I hadn't seen anything in the file I'd been given that suggested she had one. I wonder why she hadn't mentioned her at all.

I felt a little tug on my shirt, and I looked down to see a small girl no older than ten, sitting in her wheelchair beside me. She had an oxygen tank hooked on the back of her chair, and it was covered in blotches of sparkles as if someone had gone at it with some glittery nail polish.

"Are you Kacey's boyfriend?" She asked, her voice a little wheezy, but the look on her face was very serious.

I crouched down to get a little closer to her level and smiled, looking over at Kacey for any kind of direction, but she was busy. Was this one of the situations where I should just give her the simplest answer? Or was she old enough where she'd sense the lie? "I um...I'm not sure?" I finally replied, giving a little shrug.

"Why? Don't you like her?" She asked, frowning at me like I'd just committed a major faux pas. If you wanted to be in this room, you clearly had to know where your allegiances lie.

"Of course I like her, she's great." I laughed, and that seemed to mollify her, her face relaxing.

"Lisa says you look like Tom Hardy." She announced suddenly, and I heard someone, probably Lisa, call out denials from across the room. I laughed awkwardly, not knowing if that was a compliment or not.

"No way," Kacey interjected, joining the conversation, much to my relief. I stood back up and let Kacey take over, unable to match wits with this clever kid. "Everett is way taller than Tom Hardy." She gave me a gentle punch in the arm, and I smiled, wishing we weren't in a room full of children so I could kiss her and tell her just how amazing she was.

"Oh ya, you're definitely boyfriend-girlfriend." The girl decided, and I felt my cheeks heat like she had somehow known what I'd been thinking. She rolled herself away wearing a self-satisfied smile, probably to present her findings to her friend Lisa. Kacey just narrowed her eyes at me, as if the girl and I had been conspiring together against her.

Chapter 13

Everett

One by one, the kids slowly filtered out of the sunroom, either retrieved by a parent or by one of the nursing staff. Kacey made sure to say goodbye to each and every one, taking pictures whenever anyone asked. I noticed that she hadn't taken any photos for herself today, which seemed oddly strange, especially given her job. I couldn't help but ask about it while we were cleaning up the tables afterwards.

"These kids aren't props." She explained, tossing some Q-tips in a nearby trashcan. "They mean a lot to me, so I'm not about to turn around and use them for likes and follows." The kids had taken all of the makeup samples with them, so I folded up the now-empty boxes and left them at the front desk for recycling. Kacey spent a little more time with the nurses, hugging and chatting with everyone and promising to be back soon. Beth gave my cheek a little pinch, smiling like she was in on a secret that I wasn't a part of. I smiled back sheepishly, unused to this sort of motherly energy. A sharp pang of homesickness ripped through my chest. My mom had been gone for years, back before I'd even joined the Marines, but some days the pain felt still new and raw.

Kacey was looking exhausted but satisfied by the time we left what I now knew was the Long-Term Care Children's Wing of the hospital.

"I'm starving." She announced, nudging me playfully with her elbow. "Want to pick up something greasy on the way back?" I kept having to tell myself that I was working, and not just out with a beautiful girl enjoying the day. It was hard to remember that sometimes, Kacey was starting to make this feel like something more than just a job to me.

"Absolutely, the greasier the better," I replied, laughing. My phone pinged, and I stopped on the curb to check it quickly. I'd been waiting on the camera footage from the hotel to see if we could find out where the stalker went after he had disappeared down the hallway.

Jaime: *No luck man, cameras don't cover that hallway or the back stairs.*

Fuck, of course, that would be our luck. I shoved my phone back in my pocket and moved to catch up with Kacey, who was already halfway to the car.

The screech of tires caught my attention, and my adrenaline surged when I saw a car rip around the corner. It was swerving wildly, moving too fast as it drove straight towards us - straight for Kacey. Kacey was frozen like a deer in the headlights as it barrelled towards her, and I ran as fast as I could to reach her first. This was going to be too close for comfort. I lunged, hooking my arm around her waist, then used all of my weight to throw us both up on the hood of the nearest car. I twisted in mid-air, pulling her against my chest so it was me that took the brunt of the landing, mainly on my shoulder and hip. I felt the car windshield crack underneath me, and in the impact, Kacey's head slammed back into my face. Pain exploded in my nose and eye, blinding me momentarily. I could feel the car underneath us shudder as our attacker clipped the bumper, and there was the horrible sound of metal-on-metal as it skidded past us. The engine revved, and the car skidded off, turning and exiting the parking lot without slowing down.

"Everett?! Everett oh my god!" Kacey screamed, and I felt her struggling in my arms. I realized I had been clutching her tightly and I loosened my grip a little. I could only see out of one eye, and I didn't trust that the danger was truly over. I felt Kacey wiggling against me until she slipped out of my arms and down the hood of the car. I sat up quickly to stay with her and immediately regretted it when stars burst across my only working eye. The windshield creaked under me, threatening to give completely, so I shifted onto the hood until I found my footing on the ground. I touched my eye gingerly, and my fingers came back slick with blood, which couldn't be good. I knew my nose was bleeding, but something else was too it seemed. I heard footsteps approaching and grabbed for Kacey, pulling her behind me with one hand while I pulled out my gun with the other. I held it carefully at my side, using my good eye to look to see who was approaching. If only the parking lot would stop spinning so much, I could figure out what direction they were coming from.

"Kat sweetheart what happened? We heard noises, it sounded like a car crash!" The voice sounded enough like Beth that I relaxed slightly, leaning against the car for support, but I kept my gun out just in case.

"Some lunatic nearly ran us over," Kacey explained, trying to move around me. I snaked my arm around her waist, tucking her close to my hip. "Stop, we don't know if he's really gone," I told her, gritting my teeth as pain lanced across my forehead.

"They already left hun, Reggie called the police but they didn't stick around, nearly took the front gate off too." Someone said from my right. I wiped at my eye, trying to clear the blood out of it so I could see. I heard a couple of people around us gasp, and I realized I'd just flashed my gun around like an idiot.

"It's okay Beth," Kacey said quickly and slapped my hand down. "He's licensed - private security. My private security. *Could you put that away*?" She hissed. I let go of her waist and quickly stowed my gun back in the holster under my shirt.

"Alright then...well, we need to get you checked out, that's quite a nasty cut on your head," Beth replied. Despite my protests, Beth and Kacey guided me back inside the hospital, only this time it was through the main doors to the ER. We got to cut the line, thanks to Beth and the other nurses who'd surrounded us like a human shield. Soon enough I was sitting on a gurney with someone flashing a light in my eyes. Satisfied I wasn't concussed, the doctor started poking around my nose and eye socket, checking for any major breaks.

Kacey was waiting in a nearby chair, where I could see her (with my good eye). She'd been checked out first at my insistence, but aside from a decent goose egg where her head had hit my face, she had walked away without any lasting damage. I should give myself a raise - but then again, I'd let her get nearly flattened by a Subaru.

"The good news is that your nose isn't broken." The doctor announced, giving it one last poke. "But you split your eyebrow pretty good, I'll need to put in a few stitches." She put down her torture stick and grabbed a fresh tray covered in gauze and tools. "Have you had stitches before?"

"Plenty," I replied, smiling thinly. Just because I'd had them done didn't mean I particularly enjoyed needles. At least she numbed my face first, so I only felt the tug of my skin when she pulled the needle in and out. My entire face thumped along with my heartbeat, just one big aching throb. I'm sure I'd feel the rest tomorrow, but at least I hadn't cracked any ribs, only bruised them. I would be black and blue for the rest of the week, but on the bright side, I didn't need to look good to do my job. That was just a bonus.

The stitching was over quickly enough, and the doctor covered it up with a clean bandage. "Change this every six hours for the next two days." She instructed. "And take these for the swelling and the pain. Not too many though, they might make you drowsy." She handed me a bottle of pain medication I had no intention of taking, and I thanked her for her time. My one eye was swollen nearly shut, but I could make out a little bit more now that the bleeding had stopped. I was on high alert now and didn't let Kacey leave my side until we reached the car.

While we were inside the police had checked it over, declaring it safe and free from tampering or bugs. If he had known where we were going to be, he had to know what vehicle was ours and I wasn't taking any chances. They also confirmed my license and did a quick assessment of my firearm, and of course, everything had checked out. I had a sneaking suspicion that Beth had told them about my gun. She had Kacey's best interests at heart, and I couldn't fault her for that, I would've done the same.

"Give me the keys," Kacey said, blocking me from the driver's side door. I came to a stop in front of her, so close we were nearly touching.

"I'm not letting you drive my car." I laughed, but she wouldn't budge. "Do you even have a valid license?"

"I have a valid license and full vision in both eyes, so give me your keys or I'm calling us an Uber." Kacey glared up at me, feet planted and hand out, waiting.

"I can see well enough," I muttered, but I fished the keys out of my pocket to hand to her. She smirked and climbed in before I could change my mind. I tried not to cringe as she adjusted my seat, then the steering wheel, and finally the mirror. It's not that I'm a control freak, I just don't like people driving my car.

As we drove out of the parking lot I saw the damage our nasty friend had done to the front gate. I gripped the armrest as Kacey weaved in and out of traffic, seemingly comfortable behind the wheel despite not having her own vehicle. I was impressed, even after the day she'd had, that she still managed to smile and enjoy the moment.

At her insistence, we stopped at a fast food place to pick up some dinner. I had been hungry before our near-death experience, but now I was famished. We ordered way too much food once again, and Kacey loaded the bags of delicious-smelling grease on my lap before starting off back toward her condo.

Chapter 14

Kacey

I should've been exhausted, or maybe weeping uncontrollably in the corner. I definitely shouldn't feel... exhilarated. Maybe I was just in shock, and it would all hit me later tonight while I was falling asleep. I thought for sure they'd be peeling me off the pavement when I saw that car speeding towards me. Everything had happened so fast, that I didn't even have the chance to react before I was flying through the air, safely tucked against Everett's body. I thought I made out the shadowy outline of a man's form in the car as it sped past us, but I was too focused on making sure all my limbs were still attached. Even afterwards when I tried to recall any features that might help us identify the mystery assailant - likely my stalker - all I could remember was a grey blur. What if he actually was a ghost, haunting me for some perceived transgression? A ghost that could apparently drive and use modern technology.

Okay, I was definitely a little in shock.

The food helped immensely, and I started to feel more like myself after the second burger. The doctor had cleared me for any serious head injuries. Apparently, I had a thick skull, as evidenced by Everett's busted face. Feeling that the occasion warranted it - I mean, how often do you walk away from something like that in one piece - I got out my bottle of celebration scotch, which is what I called the super-fancy scotch my dad had bought me for 'special occasions only'. I poured myself a glass and looked over at Everett, still sitting at the table, looking a little worse for wear.

"Would you like one?" I asked, grabbing another glass from the cupboard. "You haven't taken your pain meds." I hadn't even seen the bottle since we got back home, and I had a sneaking suspicion that

Captain Heroic was of the 'tough it out' mindset and had left them at the hospital.

"I'm working." He reminded me, and I rolled my eyes and poured him a glass.

"I won't report you to your boss." I teased. "And it's not like my spooky pal is going to drive up five flights of stairs to try again tonight." He sighed, but it wasn't a no, and that was enough for me.

"Ice or no ice?" I asked him, I preferred mine without, but some people like cold scotch.

"Ice, but for my eye if you have some." He replied and stood up to take the glass from me. He moved slowly, as if he'd aged 60 years in the last three hours.

"For god sake, go sit on the couch before you fall and hurt yourself worse. I'll grab you an icepack." When he rolled his eye at me, I held the scotch out like I was luring a dog with a bone, and he slowly followed me into the living room, dropping onto the sofa with a heavy sigh.

"That's a good boy." I smiled and handed him his drink. He gave a little bark, smirking, and I darted away to the freezer, laughing. I had saved a few ice packs from a sprained ankle incident a few years back. As it turned out, me, plus 3-inch stilettos, plus a marble staircase equalled a midnight trip to the ER. Making my way back to the couch, I sat down beside him and took a sip of my own drink, handing over the ice pack. I watched him press it to his bad eye, now swollen completely shut and rapidly turning a horrible shade of purple. Everett winced a bit when it brushed the bandage covering his stitches. He took a sip of his drink, his healthy eyebrow raising in surprise.

"Wow, this tastes fancy." He said, leaning back on the couch. "Are you sure you should be wasting it on me?"

"It's the least I could do after destroying your face," I replied, tucking my feet up underneath me. I'd changed when we got back, my jeans were scuffed up from the car and my shirt had gotten some of Everett's blood on it. I was wearing a pair of my comfiest sweats and a loose tank top that had seen better days. My hair was pulled up in a messy bun since I'd been too hungry to bother with a shower.

"Don't worry, I'll send you an invoice for my eyebrow." He chuckled, finishing his scotch. Setting his glass down, he grabbed the icepack with his now free hand, dropping the other one to the couch where it could brush against my knee.

"Maybe you'll have one of those sexy eyebrow scars." I offered. Warmth spread through my stomach as his fingers traced absently along my leg. "You know, the ones that guys try to imitate by shaving little patches off their eyebrows?"

He laughed quietly, his head tilting back to rest against the back of the couch. "Maybe that will finally help me attract the ladies." He mused, closing his good eye. We fell into a comfortable silence, me sipping my scotch and him drawing little swirl patterns up and down my thigh. He was so vulnerable right now, and so at peace. Even after the car had driven off, he'd been so on guard, ready to keep fighting, even injured as he was. I'd never felt safer than when he pulled me tight against him, shielding me with his body, ready to defend me against the world. Heat pooled in my core, and I ached to touch him, to make him feel as good as he'd made me feel last night. I finished my drink and set my glass down on the table, then carefully so as not to jostle him, I slid my leg over his lap moving to straddle his hips.

"Hmm? What are you doing?" He asked, opening his good eye and shifting to sit up. I put a hand on his chest to push him back down.

"Ssh." I scolded, adjusting myself so my core was pressed flush against his crotch. He grunted softly, and I felt him starting to grow hard underneath me. Slowly, I undid the buttons of his shirt, trailing my fingers along his chest as I went lower. Once it was unbuttoned I pulled it down off his shoulders and tossed it on the floor. I traced the edges of his tattoo with my finger, starting behind his ear and drifting down to where it curled over his heart. Everett tossed the icepack down and grabbed for my hips, but I grabbed his wrists before they could get there.

"Ah ah ah." I smiled, pushing them down at his sides. "The doctor said to take it easy, we don't want to hurt your ribs."

"Fuck my ribs." He growled, sending a shiver of pure desire down my spine. He made to grab me again, and once more I stopped him, pressing his hands back down on the couch.

"I'll say when you can touch me." I chided and waited a moment before I let him go. This time, his hands stayed at his sides, hands curling into fists. Satisfied that he wouldn't move again, I pulled up my shirt, and he watched hungrily as I exposed my stomach inch by inch. I yanked it over my head and dropped it on the floor as well, letting him get a good look at my lilac bra. It was lacy and a demi-cup, the nicest one I owned. It squished my breasts up so it looked like they would burst out at any moment.

Everett groaned again, staring at my tits with such an intense hunger that it made me blush. That seemed to make him feral, and he shifted his hips up, pressing his hard cock against me. "Let me touch you." He begged. "I want to make you scream so loud your neighbours call to complain."

"Mm-mmm," I whispered in his ear, pressing my tits against his chest. "It's my turn still." I rocked my hips against him, rubbing myself against his length as I kissed and nipped a trail down his neck.

"Oh fuck me..." He moaned, his hands clenching at his sides. I smiled and reached my hands down between us to undo the button of his jeans.

"That's a good boy," I murmured. "Remember, no touching." I slid down off his lap, coming to rest between his legs. Giving a little tug, I pulled his jeans down and off, and they quickly joined the growing pile of clothes beside us. I could see his hard cock straining against the thin fabric of his boxers, and with one more tug, it popped free.

Fuck, he is BIG.

Everett groaned again, fists still clenched at his sides. His dick was leaking pre-cum, and with a devilish smile, I moved up between his legs and wrapped my lips around the head, flicking my tongue to lick it off.

"Sh-shit." He stammered, bucking his hips. His hands moved out towards my face, and I backed out of his reach with a coy smile.

"Are you going to behave for me?" I murmured, still holding his cock in my hand. I gave it a light squeeze to emphasize my point.

"Fuck yes, I will I promise." He whimpered and shoved his hands under his thighs to pin them down. Smiling, I bent forward and took him in my mouth again, sucking him back as far as I could manage. His guttural moan sent a shockwave of desire straight to my core, and I felt my panties begin to soak. I swirled my tongue around the head, teasing and sucking. Everett tilted his head back and closed his eyes, biting his lip. With my hand pumping up and down the base of his shaft, I swallowed him down again until his dick hit the back of my throat. He seemed to enjoy that, his hips jerking, so I did it again and again, watching his arms strain as his hands gripped the couch to keep from grabbed me.

"Oh god. Fuck Kace I'm so close..." He groaned, hips bucking, fucking my mouth with his cock. I hummed my lips around him, moaning as he jerked into me roughly. I licked up the length of his shaft, pumping him with my hand, his cock now slick with my saliva.

"That's a good boy. Now come for me." I murmured, gripping him tighter and pumping faster. His hips jerked and he moaned loudly.

"Fuck, Kacey." He grunted, and streams of warmth shot out, landing on my chest. I kept pumping, making sure that I milked his orgasm out completely. His whole body relaxed, and he was breathing hard like he'd just sprinted up three flights of stairs. I stood up between his legs, grinning wickedly. I'd reduced this strong man to begging using only my mouth, and it was an addictively powerful feeling.

I darted off to the bathroom and cleaned myself off with a damp cloth. When I got back to the living room, I saw that Everett had replaced his boxers and had dozed off, sprawled across the couch. Satisfied with my handy work - *so to speak* - I tiptoed past him to grab my shirt, already planning on a late-night rendezvous with my trusty vibrator to take care of the thrumming ache between my own legs.

I bent down to pick up my tank top and yelped as a hand hooked on my hip and pulled me down on the couch. It was eerily similar to our earlier adventures, my back pressed flush against his chest, except the couch was a lot softer than a car hood. "You were supposed to be asleep." I hissed, squirming in his grasp.

He chuckled, his breath warming the back of my neck. He held fast, his big arms like soft steel caging me against him. "All part of my dastardly trap." He murmured. One of his hands drifted up my stomach, and I wriggled as it tickled. "I've got you now, and I'm going to show you all the ways I wanted to touch you." He nipped the base of my neck gently, sucking and kissing the spot to add pleasure to the spark of pain. At the same time, his hand drifted up and landed on the front clasp of my bra. With one twist of his deft fingers, the bra popped open, and I moaned as he grabbed and kneaded my breast with his hand.

Everett shifted behind me, his knee moved up between my legs. I rocked against the pressure, heat already building in my core. "Let's see how wet you are for me." He whispered, rolling my nipple between his fingers until it hardened into a point. I hissed, arching my back as the hint of pain gave way to a jolt of pleasure. His other hand skimmed along the waistline of my sweatpants briefly before slipping underneath, where his fingers lightly stroked the damp fabric of my panties. "Hmm, looks like you enjoy being in control." He smiled against my ear before removing his fingers. I whimpered when he pulled them away, aching for him to touch me more.

"Beg me." He murmured. "Beg for my hand on your cunt." He pressed his knee between my legs and moved his hand to my other breast, teasing and pinching the nipple until I closed my eyes and moaned.

"Everett please, I need you." I pleaded, wriggling against him desperately.

"As you wish" he growled against my back. His hand dipped back into my sweatpants and inside my underwear, fingers sliding between my swollen lips. I arched into his hand, and his knee lifted my leg up to open me up to his fingers. He palmed my sex, his middle finger dipping into my folds to circle my entrance.

I whimpered pitifully, straining against his powerful arms. "Is this what you want?" Everett murmured, his finger pausing just inside the rim, his thumb moving to my clit.

"Please, yes!" I gasped, the pressure in my core threatening to spill over.

"As you wish." Two of his fingers plunged into me, pressing right into the centre of the heat building between my legs. He curled his fingers and I cried out as he hit my g-spot, unable to contain the pressure any longer. "I want to hear you scream." He kissed and sucked a spot on my neck until it burned and ached like my pussy. His fingers rubbed and circled and his thumb pressed against my throbbing clit.

I screamed loudly as I came, and he kept going, drawing the orgasm out until I had soaked his hand and my legs trembled with after-shocks.

Gently, he loosened his arms so I could roll to face him, my cheeks flushed. He smiled and kissed my lips softly. At some point I must've drifted off in his arms, but when I woke up I was alone, tucked in my own bed. My tank top and bra had been neatly placed on the dresser beside me.

Chapter 15

Everett

I was really starting to regret not taking those pain pills.

My alarm went off and I woke with a groan, every muscle in my body feeling like it had been filled with glass shards and cement. So, this is what it feels like to almost get hit by a car. I guess I can cross *actually* getting hit by a car off my list of things to try out. The swelling in my right eye had gone down a bit at least, so I could open it slightly, but I could still feel my heartbeat in my eyebrow. The bruises on my back were mild in comparison, but I'm sure they'd get worse over the coming days. I sat up gingerly and stretched, testing the limits of my range of motion. My ribs protested, but it was nothing I couldn't handle. At least Kacey was just working from home today, so I wouldn't need to gear up and move around as much.

If it had been any worse, I would be forced to call in someone to replace me, and the thought of that made my blood boil. I couldn't just sit around and do nothing while someone else did this job - *my job.* I continued to stretch, warming up my muscles to encourage better movement. I had to be the one to see this job through, I wouldn't let this guy beat me again. He'd wounded my pride, and that hurt more than all of the bruises on my body. Overnight, this job had escalated from the level of routine to very personal. And speaking of personal...

After Kacey had fallen asleep last night I hadn't wanted to move, she'd looked so peaceful in my arms, and it felt so right for her to be there. But neither of us were young enough to sleep wedged up on a couch all night, especially after the ordeal we'd faced. Thankfully, she was light enough - even dead-weight asleep - that I was able to carefully scoop her up and carry her to her bedroom. Once she was settled I'd gone back out for her clothes, leaving them on the dresser so she could find them when she woke up. I'd ached to stay and drift off to sleep next to her where I knew she was safe, but it was a bit presumptuous of me to just invite myself into her bed. Reluctantly, I crept out of her room, closed the door carefully behind me, and made my way back to my own bed.

I slid on a pair of black sweats and pulled a loose-fitting grey tee-shirt over my head before slipping out into the hallway on the hunt for coffee. I'd learned the layout of Kacey's kitchen yesterday morning, so today it only took a couple of minutes before the coffeemaker was churning happily on the counter. I snagged a fresh ice pack out of the freezer and sat down at the table to wait, the cold soothing the throbbing in my face. I should've iced it for longer last night, that was probably why the swelling was still so bad. Last night's activities had totally been worth it though, and much more healing than an icepack. I smiled to myself, thinking about how hot Kacey had looked kneeling down between my legs, ordering me around.

Good boy

A shiver went down my spine, and I felt my dick stir inside my sweats. I'd wanted to fuck her so badly last night, just bury myself in her completely until she screamed out my name. My level of restraint would be commendable if I wasn't also breaking about a hundred different rules by fooling around with a client.

The coffeemaker beeped, startling me out of the light doze I'd been slipping into. I adjusted myself and grabbed the mug I'd set out, pouring out a cup. Kacey had great taste in coffee too, I could really get used to this. Settling back down at the table, I checked my phone for messages from Jaime. Nothing new so far, and the police had also come up with jack-shit, even after yesterday's public attack. It turns out that he'd somehow obscured his license plate, likely with oil or paint, so they hadn't gotten even a partial plate from the parking lot footage. No one who witnessed the incident could ID him, or even give a basic description. It really was like this guy was a ghost. My fists clenched, and my face gave a painful throb. I forced myself to take a breath and focus on something else for the moment.

I noticed a couple of texts from my sister, but I'd get back to her later. Our mom dying seemed to have left this void of fussiness that Meagan evidently had decided she would fill, and then some. As the baby of the family, she was still way too young to be a mother hen, but she'd taken to the role with a gumption I both envied and feared. Even my dad wasn't immune to her fussing, and I worried that she used caring for her family as a way to avoid living her own life. Not that I would ever say that to her face though, she was a nightmare when she was angry.

Footsteps in the hall had me looking up from my phone, and I spotted Kacey tiptoeing past my room. I waited quietly and sipped my coffee, watching as she crept down the hall. When she finally noticed me sitting in the kitchen she let out a yelp before cursing at me. Her hair was wild from sleep, and I noticed that she was in the same sweatpants from last night, having replaced her top - but not her bra.

"Damn it Everett, I thought you were still asleep." She glared at me. "You should still be in bed, you look like you lost a fight with a bear."

"I'm still working." I reminded her, smiling as she crossed her arms over her chest. "I can't have the client wandering around while I sleep, that would defeat the whole point." That earned me an eye roll.

"Your client is in a locked apartment on the fifth floor of a secure building," Kacey replied snarkily. "Unless this creep is some sort of ninja-ghost hybrid, I think he'll have a hard time getting up here." She walked past me towards the coffeemaker, but I snagged her wrist and pulled her down onto my lap instead. Kacey gave a little squeak of protest, still irritated with me, but she calmed down slightly when I pressed a light kiss on her cheek. I tossed my icepack on the table so my hand was free to brush her hair back behind her ear.

"It's my job to keep you safe, and that means anticipating ninja-ghosts." I smiled, enjoying the feeling of her body relaxing into mine.

"Alright, fine." Kacey sighed, rolling her eyes again dramatically. She reached and brushed her fingers lightly against the bandage on my forehead, then traced a path down my cheek, pressing lightly on the little dimple that appeared whenever I smiled.

"Well if I'm going to be attacked by a ghost-ninja, I want to be well caffeinated at least." She announced, and slipped out of my grasp, darting over to the kitchen counter. I chuckled and sipped my own coffee, missing her warmth already. When she returned with her fresh mug she pulled up a chair across from me, frustratingly out of my reach, but still close enough to brush her foot against my leg. I brought the ice pack back up to my face, hoping the swelling would be down enough that I would have two fully functional eyes by tomorrow.

"Beth mentioned something to me yesterday, about your sister," I announced casually, and Kacey stiffened slightly in her chair. "I didn't know you had siblings. Does she volunteer at the hospital too?" Grief flashed across her face, and I immediately regretted opening my stupid mouth. Clearly, she hadn't mentioned her sister for a reason, and now I'd dredged something up that obviously caused her pain.

"No, Beth met my sister years ago," Kacey replied quietly, running her fingers along the sides of her coffee mug. "Her name was Felicity, and she stayed in the children's wing for a while when she was sick. Brain cancer." My stomach dropped, catching her use of past tense.

"Kacey I'm so sorry," I whispered. I reached out and rested my hand on her knee, squeezing it gently.

"It was years ago now." Kacey sighed. "We were both still kids. All she wanted to do was put on makeup and wear trashy clothes and go to the mall like her other friends, but instead, she was stuck inside that horrible grey building covered in tubes." She took a small sip of coffee, her hands trembling slightly.

"I actually started making videos just to cheer her up. I'd steal some of my mom's makeup, and do dumb things to test its "durability", like draw on my face or jump into a snow bank. She would play the videos over and over, and tell me what products were obviously 'keepers'. I started using that as a tagline just to make her laugh." She laughed softly. "After she was gone, I kept making the videos. Other people started watching them, and it made me happy to think that maybe someone else like Felicity was watching them and enjoying them too." She bit her lip, looking at the floor. "At least, that's why I used to make them. Lately...I don't know. It doesn't feel the same anymore."

I gave her knee another gentle squeeze, and Kacey smiled, her eyes glistening. "That's why I like visiting the hospital, those kids deserve to have fun and get dolled up and...and act like regular kids. It's silly, but something as simple as putting on some eyeshadow can make you feel fancy, confident, or just normal."

I couldn't believe someone this kind, this wonderful, was being hunted by some creep. When I found out who he was, I would rip his head off with my bare hands. "I'm glad you get to honour your sister that way," I told her thickly. She blushed, lifting her mug to her face, and I felt a tug of desire - a need to hold her close and kiss her until she couldn't remember being sad anymore.

With a little scoot forward, I brought my chair close to hers, making it easy to pull her forward onto my lap. Somehow, we managed to not dump her coffee on either of us - adding first-degree burns to all of my bruising would've been icing on the cake. Kacey set the mug down on the table before we pushed our luck, and shifted so she could straddle my lap. I tangled my hands through her hair and crashed my lips against hers, and she wrapped her arms around my neck to pull me close. I deepened the kiss, plunging my tongue through her already parted lips, needing to taste her. I explored her mouth with my tongue until she let out a moan that made my cock grow hard. Gripping her hair, I gave it a little tug, just enough to tip her head back, exposing her neck. I kissed greedily along her jaw and down her throat, licking and sucking and biting just enough to make her shiver in my arms. Kacey started to grind against my lap, rubbing against my entire length. I growled and recaptured her lips with mine. She sucked on my bottom lip, then gave it a little nip which made my cock jump, straining hard against my sweatpants.

"Watch it," I murmured, my hands slipping down to her breasts. "I bite back." I pulled her tank top down until one of her breasts was free. I kissed a trail down her neck until I reached it, then latched onto her nipple with my lips. I teased it with my tongue until it was a hard point, then grazed my teeth along it, making her gasp and writhe in my lap. I brought my mouth back up to hers slowly, nipping lightly at her collarbone, then her earlobe, relishing in the shiver I elicited with every brush of my teeth against her skin.

"I want you." She hissed in my ear, grinding against me. I nearly exploded right then and there. I grabbed her hips, my fingers squeezing her round and supple ass.

The doorbell rang, dousing the fire we'd started with a bucket of cold reality. Kacey froze against me, eyes wide as she stared at the door.

"You expecting someone?" I asked quietly, and slipped her off my lap, moving to the door. She shook her head at me, adjusting her top quickly to cover herself. Her lips were swollen and her cheeks were flushed with desire, and I would murder whoever was on the other side of that door just for pulling me away from that.

I motioned for her to stand behind the fridge so she wouldn't be visible from the door. Grabbing my gun off the hallway table, I flicked the safety off and moved silently to stand beside the door. With my left hand, I unlocked and unlatched it, letting it fall open a crack. Then I stepped out, gun raised, pointing it directly at the person whose hand had been poised and about to knock.

"Whoa, I didn't think you'd be *that* happy to see me. Really gross Eviebear." My sister Meagan looked at me, her nose wrinkled in mock disgust. I dropped my gun immediately, flicking the safety back on, and adjusted myself with a grimace. Apparently, the blood hadn't worked its way back to the rest of my body just yet.

"I thought they taught you how to fight with your fists in the army, not your face." She mused, eyes scanning over the damage on my face while pushing past me into the room.

Chapter 16

Kacey

I stood around the corner, furious that I was being forced to cower behind the fridge like some damsel in distress in my own damn home. I grabbed a steak knife out of the knife block and felt a little better now that I was armed. Although, if whoever it was managed to get past Everett and his gun, I probably wouldn't be overpowering them with a kitchen utensil, honestly the knife wasn't even that sharp anymore. I heard a woman's voice, which was unexpected, and then the door slammed shut. I peeked around the corner, still holding the knife, to find Everett arguing with a young woman in her early 20s. She had a short pixie-style haircut and a septum piercing. If I had to guess, her style was a sort of glam-punk blend that was currently trending among today's youth.

Today's youth? Ugh, I was starting to sound like my mother.

"Meagan, what the fuck are you doing here?" Everett snapped, putting a hand on her shoulder to stop her from moving further inside. I'd never seen him that angry before, I could practically see the smoke pouring out his ears. Meagan didn't seem fazed in the slightest by the seething man in front of her. She brushed his hand off like it was a speck of dirt, her face a mask of indifference.

"You didn't answer my texts, so I called Jaime, who can't lie for shit." She smirked as he glowered down at her. "He told me what happened yesterday, so I tracked your phone and used the security badge you gave me to get into the building. He even told me where I could find you." She pulled a thin plastic card out of her pocket, and I could see L.T.C. printed on the front.

"Remind me to fire Jaime tomorrow," Everett muttered, eyeing the badge. "And that was for when you were working as my administrative assistant, you were supposed to give that back at the end of the summer." Everett snapped, grabbing for it. She snatched it away, hiding it behind her back.

"That's beside the point. I wanted to make sure you were okay, and not bleeding out of your eyes in an alley somewhere." Meagan looked around the condo, eyebrows raised. "Obviously I shouldn't have been worried. Hi, I'm Meagan, also known as Little Sister Cole." She smiled, her eyes finding me, still half-hiding around the corner. I swear I heard Everett snarl, his jaw clenched as he glared at his sister.

"How the fuck did you track my phone?" Everett demanded, pulling the offending device out of his pocket. "Did you get Jaime to put something on it?" Meagan was walking away from him, focused on me now. I noticed her slip the ID card surreptitiously back into her pocket.

"No, *dumbass*. You put a location-sharing app on both our phones, so you could find me." She looked at me and rolled her eyes, making me snort. "It works both ways, I can see you on it too."

Okay, I had to do something before someone ended up dead in my condo -and I wasn't altogether sure it would be Meagan. "Want some coffee?" I offered, finally stepping out from behind the fridge. I gestured to the table for her to sit.

"Sure, as long as you don't stab me," Meagan replied breezily, sitting down in Everett's vacated seat. I put the knife back in the block, feeling like an idiot for grabbing it in the first place, and got a fresh mug out of the cupboard.

"She's not staying," Everett announced, stepping between us. "You are not staying." He repeated at her, eyes deadly serious. "I'm working a job, this is my client's home. You can't just waltz in here like it's no big deal! We are dealing with someone dangerous, and we don't even know who this guy is yet, or what he's capable of. He could be watching this place for all we know. You can't be seen here, it's just not safe." He threw up his hands, exasperated. I side-stepped around him, handing Meagan her coffee and then sitting down beside her. If this little speech was supposed to be making Meagan feel bad, it obviously wasn't working. If anything, she looked pensive, like she was trying to solve a riddle. I was starting to see the family resemblance, they both had the same look about them when they were working something out in their heads.

"You really think someone is just camped across the street for 24 hours a day, waiting until Kacey comes down?" Meagan asked, giving me a once over. "Not to say you aren't worth it or anything, I'm sure you are. But even creepers need to pay bills right?" I laughed, but she was right. No one could hide in the bushes for 24 hours a day watching a door. At the very least he had to eat and sleep at some point.

"He'd have to be, otherwise how could he possibly follow her everywhere she goes?" Everett snapped, running a hand over his hair, leaving it adorably dishevelled. That was the confusing part of all of this, how could he always be where I was unless he was literally watching me 24/7? And how could he watch me 24/7 if he was a human being? Our ghost-ninja hypothesis was getting more and more believable.

"Boy, you really aren't the tech brains at your operation are you?" Meagan sighed and held up her phone. "Think, Eviebear. At any moment, you can see where I am anywhere in the world, as long as my phone is on."

"Sure, fine." He sighed. "But I set that up on your phone. It's not like Kacey handed her phone to a stranger and waited patiently for them to install the right software on it." They both looked at me for confirmation, and I hesitated, biting my lip.

If I really thought about it, how many times had I given someone my phone to take a picture, or handed it over to let them enter their insta handle? How many times had I left my phone on the table to do a shot with my friends? The opportunities had been there, plentiful thanks to my inherent trust in the kindness of strangers. I felt the colour drain from my face. "Oh my god, what if he did put something on my phone?" I looked at the piece of technology sitting on the table in front of me, seized with the violent urge to shove it in the garbage disposal.

Meagan reacted quicker, she snatched it up off the table and quickly shut it off like she was defusing a bomb. She dropped it back on the table, and all three of us stared at it like it might actually start smoking.

"Okay...now what?" I asked quietly, the cold ache of dread seeping back into my stomach.

"Got a hammer?" Meagan suggested, and Everett gave her a small shove, rolling his eyes.

"Now, I call the *tech brains* of my operation and see how we find out if there's something tracking you on here," Everett replied, pulling out his own phone to make the call. Meagan and I listened in as Jaime walked Everett through the troubleshooting process. He had him turn my phone back on, and then plug it into his laptop. Jaime then used some remote wizardry to run diagnostics on the phone.

Technical genius was not very exciting to watch, especially when the genius in question wasn't even in the room. After over an hour of huddling around the table, watching the laptop blink as different windows popped up and closed, I was starting to think that the garbage disposal was still the best course of action. He couldn't track a phone that no longer existed, right?

"Alright guys, I found it." Jaime's voice crackled through the speaker of Everett's phone. "He was very careful, it was hidden in your inactive app settings." I had no idea what that meant, but I could've kissed Jaime at that moment.

"That's great! Can you please delete it, wipe the whole phone if you have to." I replied earnestly, desperate to exorcise this ghoul from my phone.

"Wait hold on!" Meagan jumped up, startling both Everett and I. "Don't remove it just yet." I could see her mind working furiously behind her calculating brown eyes. I had a feeling that I wasn't going to like whatever plan she was concocting.

"What're you thinking Meg?" Everett asked, brow creased, he seemed to feel the same way as I did. I wonder how many times Meagan's plans had gotten him, or both of them, into trouble.

"What if - now, hear me out first before you freak out." She glared at Everett, and he put his hands up in mock surrender. "We leave the tracker on for now. He doesn't know that we know it's there, so now we are ahead of the game. We stir shit up with something that'll really piss him off, and then we lure that fucker out and catch him once and for all!" She slapped her hands on the table for emphasis. So, it wasn't terrible, as far as ideas go. But there was a lot that could go wrong, and I don't think she'd planned any contingencies just yet.

"First off, since when is it *we*?" Everett replied, raising an eyebrow at her, and Meagan shot back a dirty look. "Secondly...alright, it's not the worst plan. But, even if we do manage to lure him out, how will I know who he even is? We still don't know what he looks like." He ran a hand through his hair in frustration.

"Maybe I can help with that." Jaime piped up, and we all looked down at Everett's phone. I had forgotten we had a fourth person attending this little meeting. "Now that I found the trace, I can enable the two-way function to see him. Then, when he gets close to you, I can call his number."

"Wait. You have his fucking number?" Everett asked in disbelief.

"Okay, so if anyone - say, a lawyer or a police officer asks - then no, I do not have his number. Because pulling that information from third-party app data is highly illegal." Jaime replied quickly, and Everett rolled his eyes. "But, if you guys just happen to see some creepy-looking guy getting a wrong number call right as they are approaching you...well let's just chalk it up to fortuitous timing."

"I'm good with that." Meagan announced, "You good with that Eviebear?"

"I was in the bathroom for this part of the conversation and didn't hear my employee say anything about illegal activities," Everett muttered. "But yes, that plan works then. Kace, you've got that dinner thing tomorrow right?"

I groaned, having forgotten about that in all the chaos surrounding me at the moment. "Yes, it's part two of the damn product launch." I sighed. I needed to find a clean dress for tomorrow I guess. At least Alexis would be there too, people always talked to her more so I was able to just stand there and look pretty.

"Perfect!" Meagan clapped her hands together, looking like an evil genius. "Alrighty, now the bait..." She pursed her lips, thinking. This was the part that made my chest tighten. I didn't want to piss off the guy who had already tried to run us over with his car.

"He was pretty mad when he saw us ki - uh, together in the hallway." Everett offered, looking awkward. I noticed a hint of colour in his cheeks, and it made me smile to see him blush.

"Ooh, perf." Meagan smiled, oblivious to his discomfort. "Kacey, what if you posted a soft launch? That would definitely get his attention." She took a sip of her coffee, looking proud of herself.

"That could work I guess." I mused, chewing on my lip. "But he already knows about Everett or thinks he does at least. Would that be enough, do you think?" Or would that be too much, and it forces him to retaliate with something worse than just a car?

"I'm sorry, but what the fuck is a soft-launch?" Everett asked, and Meagan and I both laughed, which made him frown.

"Sorry *Grandpa*, I forgot you don't speak internet." Meagan rolled her eyes, and he swatted at her. "A soft launch is when someone subtly drops news of their new relationship online, you know, making it official. Except with a soft launch, it's just a subtle picture. Something like...I don't know, two plates on the dinner table, or holding hands or something. You wouldn't need to show your face." She grimaced at his bruises like he'd gotten them purposefully just to annoy her.

"Oh, so like an engagement announcement, but the groom is anonymous?" Everett asked, making Meagan snort, but then she thought on it for a moment.

"Now that's an idea." She smiled, looking positively devious. "Here, try this." She worked a ring off her finger, dropping it into my palm with a self-satisfied "Ta-dah!"

"Why the fuck do you have an engagement ring, Meagan?" Everett demanded as I tested the size carefully on my own finger.

"It's for when I tell guys that I have a fiancé. This way they actually believe me and stop hitting on me." She replied breezily. "Oh good it fits!" She grabbed my hand, nearly pulling me off the chair just so she could see it better under the light. "Isn't it *gorg*? I got it from a pawn shop for practically nothing."

"It sure is...something," I murmured. It really was beautiful - clearly vintage, it had a dark emerald centre stone, with clusters of diamonds on either side. I looked up at Everett, trying to gauge his thoughts. "Are you okay with being fake engaged for a day or two?" I asked softly.

"Of course, whatever it takes." He smiled, flashing his dimple. Meagan clapped her hands, beyond thrilled that we were using her plan.

Chapter 17

Everett

It took a little longer for Jaime to finish up with Kacey's phone, but she didn't seem too eager to get it back. Once we finished up with that call, Kacey left to call Alexis and fill her in on the plan. Apparently, an engagement soft launch would cause quite a stir across her socials, so it was best for Alexis to be prepared. While she dealt with the business side of things, I was left to clean up the familial side, mainly trying to convince Meagan to leave. She finally did, but only after I promised to let her know how the plan went with a full play-by-play. Meagan was all smiles as she walked out of the condo - she was always happiest when everything was going exactly as she planned. I was just re-locking the door as Kacey finished up her call, and she came out of her room looking tired. I saw her twisting the unfamiliar ring around her finger nervously, unused to the feel of it just yet.

"Ready to be engaged?" She laughed nervously, but I could tell she felt uncomfortable. Was I ready? I smiled back at her. Of course, I wanted to catch this guy, and I knew that this was just bait and it wasn't real. If it was real, you'd better believe that there would have been an epic proposal, maybe something involving a sky-writer. But what had been growing between us the last few days...that was starting to feel very real. What would happen once this was all over? Would I just...send her a bill and move on with my life?

Apparently, setting up for the perfect 'casual photo' took a lot of work. I let Kacey drag me all around her living room, looking for 'good light'- as she put it. Once we found the light, she had me hold out my hand, laying hers on top so the ring was centre-stage. I held as still as I could, letting her mould me into the right pose. Satisfied with the set-up, Kacey then took about a hundred photos, all at slightly different angles and from slightly different distances, adjusting the focus and the lighting with each one. My arm was actually starting to get sore by the time she declared she'd gotten it. Who knew that a simple photo for social media could be so complicated?

Getting the photo was only the first step of the process evidently, so we moved on to step 2, which involved her laptop. Opting for comfort over practicality, we headed into her room to work. Kacey sat down on the bed and got cozy with her laptop propped on her stomach. I sprawled across the foot of her bed like a dog, resting my eyes while I listened to her type. There was a soothing sort of peace that settled around us, her working quietly while I dozed close by. Even when we weren't talking, it was just nice to have her near.

"There," Kacey announced, and I blinked open my eyes, unsure of how much time had passed. "It's live now, everyone can see it." She flipped her laptop around so I could see too. The caption under the photo read *Speak now or forever hold your peace.* Well, if the picture didn't piss him off, the deliberate taunt of the caption sure would. My stomach twisted, uneasy now that the trap had been set. I hated that all we could do now was wait and see if he took the bait.

"That should definitely get his attention," I murmured. Kacey groaned, slumping back down with her laptop. When she'd resumed typing, I shifted onto my side and took one of her feet in my hands. I began to massage it lightly, working my thumbs in little circles across the sole.

"Mmm...that feels nice." Kacey purred, and I smiled, continuing my ministrations. After I while I switched to her other foot, and I could feel her start to relax, her muscles becoming more pliant under my hands. Kacey kept working, but I could hear her pausing every so often, and when I hit one particular spot she closed her eyes and hissed out a breath between her teeth.

"Aren't you supposed to be resting?" She asked glancing at me over her laptop. Her eyes narrowed, but her cheeks were flushed, and clearly, she'd been enjoying the massage.

"I am resting, I'm even lying down, see?" I smirked back, gesturing at my legs stretched out on the bed. Once her head disappeared back behind her laptop, I continued working my hands up to her calf.

Kacey stayed quiet for a while, and I made my way slowly upwards, massaging her knees before starting on her thighs. I took my time, focusing on each muscle and working any tension out with my fingers. I heard her breath hitch when my hand slid up her inner thigh, and I paused, no longer hearing her typing.

"Aren't you supposed to be working?" I asked her coyly, earning myself a dirty look from over the top of the laptop.

"I'm trying to work, but it's a little hard to concentrate when you're doing that." Kacey bit back, before settling back down. "I still need to reply to three more emails. And I should order us something to eat. Are you hungry yet?"

"Starving," I growled, and slipped my hands up to her hips, hooking my fingers around her waistband. One swift tug and her sweatpants came down, a second tug and they were completely off. Kacey yelped, clutching her laptop before it slid off onto the floor. I tossed her pants to the side of the bed, as she glared at me, flustered, her lips parted and ready to scold me.

"Don't mind me." I smiled, tugging her panties down as well. "Just keep working." She responded with an exasperated sigh and propped her laptop back up on her stomach defiantly.

Chuckling, I grasped one of her legs and hoisted it up in the air, hooking her knee over my shoulder. I began pressing kisses along her inner thigh, sucking and grazing my teeth against her skin until she started to squirm underneath me. "Focus on your work." I teased, putting my hands on her hips to hold her still. I heard the clicking of keys on the keyboard, but they were a lot slower than they were before, and there was a long pause between clicks every time I pressed my lips to her skin.

With agonizing slowness, I worked on her other thigh, using my tongue to draw a line up towards her core. I'd give her the occasional nip, loving how her hips would buck in response. I held her firmly, not allowing her to wiggle away from me. I could see her getting wet, moisture beginning to pool between her thighs. Kacey wasn't typing anymore, although her laptop was still in her hands. I could hear her breathing quickly in small shuddering bursts.

"I've been wanting to taste you for days," I murmured. "I bet you're fucking delicious." I nestled deep between her thighs, running my tongue up along the full length of her slit. Kacey rocked her hips, a soft whimper escaping her throat. I gripped her ass with both hands, pinning her against my mouth, and dipped my tongue between her folds, tasting her hot desire. She moaned loudly when my tongue plunged inside her pussy, and her laptop dropped, forgotten, onto the bed beside her. I replaced my tongue with two fingers, shifting my mouth up to focus on her clit. My dick was painfully hard, and I pushed my hips down against the bed, the pressure only a shadow of what I craved. I pulled her sensitive bud into my mouth, sucking until she was writhing beneath me, riding my face. She tangled her hands in my hair, pulling me tight against her pussy, her thighs starting to clench around my head. I curled my fingers against her g-spot, swirling my tongue around her clit deftly before grasping it between my teeth.

"Everett!" Kacey cried out, thighs clenching. Her whole ass rose off the bed as she orgasmed, soaking my hand with her juices. I kept stroking with my fingers, drawing it out until she collapsed onto the bed, her leg heavy and trembling on my shoulder. Letting her leg drop to the bed, I pulled myself up until I was level with her face, admiring how sexy she looked, with her eyes half closed and lips parted in desire. I kissed her, letting her taste herself on my lips. She fisted a hand in my shirt, deepening the kiss.

"I want you inside me." Kacey moaned against my lips. "Now!"

"As you wish," I whispered, tearing myself away from her just long enough to kick off my sweatpants and boxers, groaning when my dick popped free. Kacey grabbed my shirt collar with both hands and pulled me down on top of her once more. "I need to grab a condom" I murmured, but she wouldn't loosen her grip, kissing down my neck.

"I'm on birth control, it's fine." She replied, hands moving down to pull at my hips, begging me to close the space between us. Her need drove me wild, and it was taking all of my control to pace myself and not just devour her completely.

I nestled my hips between her thighs, lining the head of my cock with her slick entrance. When I didn't move further, she groaned in frustration, digging her nails into my sides impatiently. I sank into her just enough to dip the head of my cock in her folds, then I stopped once again. I felt her walls clench around me, and she all but snarled in my ear. The heat between us was threatening to ignite and burn the condo down around us. I kissed her roughly, my tongue exploring her mouth as she arched and writhed beneath me.

"Is this what you want?" I murmured in her ear, teasing her entrance with my cock.

"Yes, please Everett! Fuck me!" Kacey begged, arching underneath me. I smiled and kissed her again.

"As you wish." I plunged all the way inside of her, letting out a ragged groan as I felt her muscles clench tightly around me. Kacey cried out and dug her nails into my back, urging me on. Fuck, I wouldn't hold out much longer if she kept making noises like that. I rocked my hips, thrusting into her slowly at first, pulling almost entirely out before plunging back in, burying myself into her slick core again and again. She wrapped her legs around me, and I could feel her pussy starting to clench as an orgasm built. I started to thrust faster, harder and reached down to toy with her clit. Kacey screamed as the release tore through her, her pussy spasming and clamping down on my cock. I moaned and came hard as I continued to thrust into her, milking her orgasm until we were both spent.

Breathing hard, I lowered myself to the bed, careful not to crush her laptop, which had gotten lost somewhere in the covers. Kacey curled up in my arms, her eyes closing, and I brushed my lips against her forehead. After the job was finished, I wasn't sure how I would just walk away from all of this.

Chapter 18

Kacey

"Stop squirming, or I'll take your eye out!" I snapped, as Everett once again flinched away from my hands. For a big strong man, he could sure act like a fussy toddler sometimes.

"I could do this myself." He groused. I had him slouching in one of the kitchen chairs - the only way I could get eye-level with him easily - and was trying to change the bandage over stitches, but the glue from the bandage was sticking to his eyebrow hair. I was currently trying to remove the bandage while avoiding removing his eyebrow in the process. I could've been finished by now, but Everett was a terrible patient and refused to hold still. We had already suffered a few casualties, any more and he was going to be looking permanently surprised for a few weeks.

"If I let you do this, you'd rip your eyebrow clean off, and I refuse to be engaged to a man with only one eyebrow," I told him sharply and leaned forward to start again. I was using a Q-tip and some rubbing alcohol to carefully dislodge the bandage, and it was slowly but surely coming off, except...

"Would you quit that already!" I tapped him on the nose with the Q-tip, his hands once again creeping up under my shirt. "Do I need to get a spray bottle?"

"You're the one sitting on my lap," Everett smirked, his hands tickling my waist.

"I will tie your hands behind your back if you can't hold still." I threatened, but it had the opposite effect of what I intended. His eyes lit up with a hungry gleam, and I let out an exasperated sigh. "You need to look at least somewhat presentable tonight, and your face is already black and blue. Let's not add a sharpie eyebrow to that list."

"Alright, alright, fine." He sighed, still grinning. He brought his hands behind his back, lacing his fingers together. "Happy?"

Once he settled down, I was able to make quick work of the bandage. Once I had the last of it peeled off, I handed him my small mirror so he could check it himself. I had no idea what stitches were supposed to look like, or how to tell if they were infected. Even healing properly they still looked gross to me. After some careful inspection, Everett declared that he didn't need to put a new bandage on right away, since the stitches were starting to heal already. At least without the bandage, all we had to worry about was the awful bruise still covering half his face. Everett had vehemently denied letting me use makeup to cover some of the bruising, insisting that it made him look dashing and mysterious. I told him it looked like he'd walked into a door frame, but I decided not to fight him on this one. If he couldn't hold still to take off a bandage, I can't imagine how irritating he would be if I came at him with the concealer.

I was getting more and more nervous about the event tonight and was starting to regret agreeing to go. How had that shadowy creep following me reacted when he saw the post? Everett confirmed that he hadn't posted any photos of me since it went up, and I wasn't sure if that was a good or bad sign. I just hoped that it would all be over after tonight. I had bigger things to worry about.

Things like what Everett would do when this was all over. He obviously wouldn't need to stick around once we caught the guy and there was no longer any threat to my safety. Would he want to continue with...whatever this was that was happening between us? He was pretending to be engaged to me, was it possible to just roll that back and casually date for a while afterwards? Would he even want to? It was quite possible that this was all just about convenience - we were both stuck together so might as well make the best of it. But I didn't feel that way, and I wasn't sure how to let him know that I wanted something more than that.

I wasn't normally such a disaster when it came to work events, but my nerves had me absolutely frazzled. Getting ready was an ordeal, and I must've tried on every dress I owned twice before I finally settled on one I didn't despise. In my haste to make up for lost time I nearly blinded myself with my mascara brush because my hands were shaking. I took my time after that near miss because at least one of us should have two working eyes. Of course, this meant that once again we were running late to the event, and I hustled out into the kitchen when I was finally finished, my heels clacking on the tile.

"Okay, I'm ready! Let's get moving." I announced, giving Everett a quick once over. He was already waiting in his usual perch against the kitchen counter, hands in his pockets when I walked in. He looked like a gangster in his dark suit and burgundy dress shirt, which somehow complimented the bruises around his eye. Damn it, he was right, the bruises did make him look mysterious. It was truly unbelievable how he could look so effortlessly sexy.

Meanwhile, I was already second-guessing my dress and my eye still stung from being jabbed. He looked up as I approached, his eyes - now both open at least - roving up and down my body in a way that made me blush. I twisted my ring nervously, and he stalked towards me like a puma. Everett stopped just short of me, his body nearly pressed against mine. He still towered over me, even with my heels on, but that had never stopped him before. He leaned down and pressed a kiss against my lips, his fingers tracing along my jaw. Heat pooled in my stomach, and I moved to deepen the kiss, but he pulled back abruptly with a smirk.

"We should get going, we don't want to be late." He said casually, and I glared at him. Everett offered me his arm, ever the gentleman, and I conceded, leaning into his warmth. He would keep me safe tonight, no matter what happened.

Chapter 19

Everett

I'd gone over the plan with Jaime at least a dozen times that day, and by the time we'd arrived at the venue, I was feeling almost confident in our chances of success. Jaime would be watching us from the moment we left, tracking both Kacey and I's phones. I opted to wear an earpiece tonight, which I normally saved for when I was working in a team of two or more people. I didn't want to risk missing a text from Jaime, so I shoved the tiny device into my ear. At least with my height, only someone as tall as me would be able to see it, and even then it could be mistaken for a hearing aid - because who actually wore an earpiece outside of a spy movie? Jaime would let me know when our perp was on the move. Once he was close enough that his dot was on top of ours, Jaime would alert me and then start calling him from a spoofed number. Now, as long as there weren't too many people taking calls at this event tonight, our plan should be pretty foolproof.

I hadn't told Kacey this part, but I was also counting on the fact that the stalker would see me as his main target, now that I had 'laid claim' to the object of his affection. I preferred to be the one in harm's way, especially since I was the one who could wear a kevlar vest under my outfit. It wouldn't stop a headshot, or anything bigger than a handgun, but the thin layer of armour on my chest and back could also mean the difference between a trip to the hospital and a trip to the morgue. The vest itself was a bit constricting, and it pushed painfully against the bruises on my back whenever I twisted, but a gunshot wound hurt a lot worse, so I kept it on.

There was no way that Kacey would be able to wear a vest under her outfit, especially not the one she was wearing tonight. The sleek blue dress with see-through lace running up along both sides made it apparent just how little she could wear underneath it. A slit ran up along her left thigh, exposing even more skin when she walked. It took all of my effort to keep my hands to myself, and I settled for a kiss before I lost my mind completely and made us both very late for the dinner.

"Tell Kacey hi from me!" Jaime had chirped in my ear, and I ignored him, already regretting the earpiece. There was unfortunately no mute option on my end, short of taking it out, so I was stuck with his little voice in my head for the whole evening. It was a good deterrent for the dirty thoughts running through my head, knowing that he'd hear everything if I decided to act on my carnal impulses with Kacey at any point in the evening.

The drive over was quick enough, I let Jaime know we were on the move and he confirmed that both our phones were tracking as they should. I kept one hand on the wheel, letting the other hand rest on Kacey's thigh. She placed her hand on top of mine, and I could feel her new ring rubbing against my finger. At least pretending to be engaged gave me an excuse to keep her close tonight, there was no way I'd be losing her in the crowd this time. I gave her leg a gentle squeeze, reassuring myself once more that this was a good plan, and nothing would go wrong.

The hotel venue for this event had valet parking so we were able to stop right out front, avoiding any potential for parking lot adventures. I handed my keys to one of the waiting valets and escorted Kacey inside, where the party was already in full swing. A server showed us to our assigned places, weaving us through the tables until we spotted Alexis, already seated with a drink in her hand.

"Lexi!" Kacey exclaimed, rushing over to give her manager a hug.

"Kace! Congratulations!" Alexis announced loudly, shooting me a wink over Kacey's shoulder. She grabbed Kacey's hand to get a better look at the ring. Fake engagement or not, it still required scrutiny, evidently. They stood with their heads bent together, whispering for a few minutes while I took my seat. It must've passed inspection, because they quickly joined me, sharing a grin. Kacey leaned over and gave me a quick peck on the cheek, and I moved my chair slightly so that I could drape my arm over her shoulder.

A server passed us, offering glasses of champagne. I snagged one, handing it to Kacey who smiled an acknowledgement. I wouldn't be having any tonight, as usual, but I felt that Kacey might benefit from it, I could see her hands shaking with nerves.

Soon after we arrived, Jaime updated me to say that our perp was on the move, heading in our direction. I kept my eyes on the main door, guests and servers trickling in and out consistently throughout the evening. People dropped by our table in a steady stream that was starting to put my teeth on edge. It was impossible to keep track of who was moving in and out of the room while also attempting small talk with over a dozen people.

Everyone wanted to offer their congratulations to Kacey, and me by extension. Luckily I was the unimportant, anonymous suitor, so that meant my part of the conversation was brief. Few guests tried to engage me in direct conversation, maybe it was the menacing-looking bruise on my face that scared them away. Several people clearly just used the opportunity as an excuse to ask Kacey about promotional opportunities with the wedding. Alexis handled these questions tactfully, telling everyone that we were still in the early stages of planning and weren't sure of any details just yet. I wonder what the backlash would be like when Kacey had to announce our 'break-up' after this ordeal was over. I didn't understand how a wedding could even have promotional opportunities. Would she stand up at the altar with a little sign beside her saying *Dress by Valentina*? Even after getting Kacey to explain it to me, I still didn't quite understand what her job entailed. I got the feeling that even the people doing this job didn't always fully understand it.

Once dinner was served the visitors to our table decreased, which I was extremely thankful for. I continued to watch the door, barely touching my food. Kacey let me be, talking mostly with Alexis and the other people at our table while eating her meal. I snagged another glass of champagne for her when I saw she'd run out, earning me another kiss on the cheek. If I hadn't been on the lookout for a crazed stalker, this could've been a really lovely evening. Maybe once this was all behind us, I could take Kacey out for a romantic meal where I could also have some champagne and stare at her all evening, instead of the exit. A man can dream, right?

Jaime announced that he'd arrived just as dinner service ended, and I sat up straighter in my seat, eyes glued to the doorway. Jaime wouldn't be able to tell me where exactly he was in the building, but he should be able to warn us once he was within 10 to 15 feet of us, when our little dots started overlapping on his screen.

Kacey put her hand on my thigh, and I forced my attention back to the table. "They're asking for some photos of a few of us, just outside in the lobby." She told me quietly. "Is that okay?" Not the ideal situation, but she was here to work, so we would make it work.

"Of course." I nodded smiling gently, and followed her lead as we made our way towards the front of the room. I stayed close behind Kacey, my fingers grazing her lower back. I couldn't risk getting separated from her, especially when we knew he was close.

"Whoa whoa, you guys are almost on top of him!" Jaime suddenly exclaimed in my ear. I stopped dead, my eyes scanning the room. Someone bumped my arm, forcing their way past me, and I reluctantly continued moving forward so I wasn't blocking the flow of traffic. Once we were out past the doors I pulled Kacey aside, close to one of the walls of the lobby, tucking her between me and the wall while I scanned the room. There were hardly any people milling around in the lobby, just a couple of hotel workers and a server on their break. I didn't see anyone who looked suspicious or overly interested in Kacey, but we already knew he could hide in plain site so I kept my guard up.

"Okay man, start calling him," I whispered to Jaime, looking around the room. The lobby was quieter than the dining room, so it would be easier to spot if someone was answering their phone. I could feel the adrenaline pumping through my veins, and my heart was starting to race with anticipation.

"That's weird," Kacey murmured, also looking around. "I thought they were already out here waiting for me." She pulled out her phone, typing furiously.

"Who?" I asked, running my hand across my face. Why was I sweating so much? And why was it so bright in this damn room? I squinted and blinked rapidly, trying to clear up my eyes. Something didn't feel right. I looked around, but everything seemed to blur as soon as I tried to focus on it.

"One of the event coordinators texted to ask for pictures with everyone, they said they were all waiting out here for me," Kacey replied, looking up from her phone. "Everett? Are you okay?" Her voice sounded concerned all of a sudden.

I blinked again, but the room stayed blurry. I took a step back and everything started to tilt sharply to the left. I felt Kacey grab my arm to steady me, just as my knees buckled. I slid down the wall to the floor, my legs no longer responding to my brain's directions.

"Some..thing's wrong," I mumbled, fighting to stay conscious. Was this a heart attack? I wasn't sure, I had never had one before. "Go find 'lexis." I tried to Kacey, even though I could barely make out her face anymore as she crouched in front of me, touching my cheek. I could hear her phone ringing, probably the event coordinator trying to find her. I hoped my dying wouldn't get her in trouble at work.

"Call for help! We need an ambulance, he's sick! Please!" Kacey called out to someone, but I couldn't see who it was. Why wasn't she answering her damn phone? That sound was going to drive me crazy, she should just answer it and tell them to call back later.

"He's not picking up, but he's right on top of you!" Jaime told me. When had Jaime gotten here? Shouldn't he be at the office? My brain was desperately trying to keep my thoughts together, but they kept breaking apart, the pieces floating away into the night. I couldn't tell if I was even awake anymore, maybe I was just dreaming this, back in bed with Kacey after a relaxing evening together.

Was I dying? I grabbed for my gun, but the movement tipped me over and I slumped down to the ground. My arms were too weak to break my fall, but it didn't seem to hurt, even when my bruised face smacked into the floor. This felt like a good place to lay down for a while, I was so tired, and the tile was so cool against my burning skin.

If only that phone would stop ringing, that thing was grating on my nerves. Wait, weren't we waiting for a phone call?

"Kace...Run!" I tried shouting at her, fighting around the cotton balls that had filled my mouth.

"RUN!" I saw a blue shape moving away from me, but then another large shape grabbed it, pulling it - pulling Kacey - away from me.

The last thing I heard before I lost consciousness was her terrified scream.

Chapter 20

Everett

"Everett? Everett! What's going on man, fucking answer me!" Who was fucking shouting at me? I pressed my face against my pillow, but it was weirdly hard, and cold. Had someone replaced my pillow with a rock? Someone was shaking my arm violently, the movement making my head throb. Why were so many people in my bedroom? How had I gotten home last night?

I finally opened my eyes, or my eye rather, wincing as the light increased the throbbing in my brain. My face felt sticky, and I had to move slowly to peel it up off the floor. Alexis was crouched over me, white as a ghost, still shaking my arm. I sat up quickly - too quickly - and a wave of nausea had my stomach clenching violently. There were a lot more people in the lobby now, and I could see police officers milling in the crowd.

"Where's Kacey?" I demanded, voice cracking. My throat felt like I'd swallowed sandpaper. I wiped my hand over my eye, and it came away sticky with congealed blood. I touched my eyebrow and winced as pain sliced across my face. It felt like one of my stitches had popped, which explained the blood on my face. I just couldn't remember what I had done to reopen it in the first place.

"Everett, thank god!" Jaime shouted in my ear, and I winced at the volume. "You weren't answering, and then I saw Kacey and the perp take off in the same direction. I called the police to your location, but they were already gone by the time they showed up."

"God damn it." I snarled and used the wall for support as I made my way to my feet. My body creaked in protest, too old to be sleeping on marble floors for any length of time. "I think that fucker drugged me." I rubbed my arm, trying to replay what had happened that evening. "There was a person who bumped into me earlier, just before we left the dining room. That could've been him. He must've jabbed me with something and then waited until I was down to grab her." I rubbed my eyes, trying to clear my head. "How long was I out for?"

"You went quiet for over an hour man," Jaime replied softly. So he had at least an hour's head start, I would have to move fast if I had any hope of catching up to them.

"Fuck!" I snarled, startling Alexis, who was still at my side. At least whatever it was hadn't knocked me out for longer, or worse. Maybe he'd misjudged the dosage, or maybe he just figured that I'd never be able to find him if and when I woke up.

"I need to find her," I muttered. "Jaime, can you tell me which way they went?" I stretched my shoulders, still feeling out of sorts in my own body. I checked that my gun was still in its proper place, furious that I'd never even managed to unclip it from the holster. My blood boiled at the idea that he'd gotten the jump on me once more. I was so full of rage, there was no telling what I'd do when I finally got my hands on him. If he hurt so much as one hair on Kacey's head...No, I couldn't think about that right now.

"Kacey must still have her phone," Jaime told me suddenly. "I can see both of their dots heading east, so far they haven't left downtown though. I'll text you the street info." I felt my phone start to vibrate as he spoke. I quickly scanned the lobby, figuring out my escape route.

"Everett? The police want to talk to you." Alexis reappeared at my side - I hadn't even noticed when she'd left. "There are EMT's waiting outside to take you to the hospital to get checked out." She had clearly been crying, her eyes red and puffy. I would've tried to comfort her, but I didn't have the time right now, not when every second could make a difference for Kacey.

"I'm fine" I replied quickly. "I'll drive myself there." After I found Kacey - I added silently. I wasn't wasting precious time with a medical detour. I slipped around the crowd, stumbling a bit as my feet remembered how to walk.

Alexis followed after me, distressed. "Please Everett, you need to tell them what happened, they need to know where to start looking for Kacey!" Right, they'd cover a lot more ground than I could on my own, but they'd also slow me down if I had to wait around to talk to them.

"I'll call Sergeant Jeffreys on the way," I told her, weaving around a particularly large group in front of the door. She let me go, and I felt momentarily bad for brushing her off. I'd make sure to apologize to her after I found Kacey.

"Jaime, call Sergeant Jeffreys, let him know you're tracking Kacey's location and have him send units after them." I flagged down one of the valets and handed him my ticket. Jaime grunted a quick acknowledgment, and I felt my phone vibrate again. I pulled out my phone as the valet pulled my car around, checking quickly through the directions Jaime had sent me, trying to predict where this guy was headed next. I realized I had another new notification, and ice flooded my veins. I opened it to find a new post from our perp.

The picture was of Kacey, tied up and shoved in the trunk of a car. My gut clenched, seeing the fear in her eyes. The caption read *She's Mine Now.*

Chapter 21

Kacey

I shivered, wishing I had worn a coat to the event tonight. Of course, I hadn't foreseen being shoved in the trunk of a car, so warmth hadn't been my top priority when I was getting dressed today. My shoulder was starting to ache, and I tried to shift around to get some relief when I felt something hard digging into my boob. Holy shit, I still had my phone! When Everett had started to collapse in the lobby, I'd shoved it into my bra to free up my hands. By some miracle, it hadn't fallen out in the ensuing struggle. At least one thing had gone my way tonight.

Oh god, Everett...My momentary happiness about the phone fizzled out, letting the panic seep back into my chest. Please, please, don't let him be dead...

He'd gone so pale, even after the car incident, he hadn't looked that bad. I didn't know what to do, so I'd just called out to the nearest person for help. Maybe he had a heart attack or something like a stroke. I should've tried doing CPR, but instead, I'd just stood there like an idiot. He had started mumbling something to me, but I couldn't understand what he was saying until he had said one thing with terrifying clarity.

Kace...Run!

It had taken me a second to process what he was saying, shock rooting me to the ground. But Everett would have only told me to run for one reason.

Run!

I had turned to run back into the dining room, figuring I'd be safest in the crowd, but someone had stepped in front of me, blocking my path. His phone had been going off in his hand, and I'd watched as he silenced it with a press of a button. "Wrong number." He told me, pocketing it with a shrug. "Come on Kacey, let's go." The hairs on the back of my neck had stood up at the sound of my name. When he had grabbed at my arm, I'd back-peddled quickly, yanking it out of his reach. My chest had begun to tighten as panic filled my lungs. I had never seen this man before - not that I could recall, at least. But I knew him deep in my bones. This was the man who had been haunting me.

"No." I'd whispered, fear catching in my throat, and that's when he pulled a knife out of his jacket. I knew wasn't going to be able to fight my way out of this, not when he had a weapon and I had...nothing. We should've thought this through more, we hinged this whole plan on Everett being alive to protect me, and I had never given any thought about how to protect myself.

"I'm here to rescue you, baby, you're safe now." He had told me, smiling as his eyes lit up with a terrifyingly manic energy. He had lunged suddenly just as I'd tried to make a break for the dining room. He'd grab me around the waist, and I had tried to scream as loudly as I could before he put the knife against my throat. "Be a doll and quiet down." He'd whispered in my ear. "We're going to go for a drive."

With brutal efficiency, he had pulled me to a set of stairs leading down to an underground parkade. I'd stumbled trying to keep up, but he held onto me with a bruising strength, the knife never leaving my throat. When we'd finally reached his car, he'd forced me into the trunk and then had me tie my feet together. Only when I was finished did he finally put the knife away so he could tie my hands behind my back. Then as an added safeguard, he'd used some more rope to connect my hands and feet - forcing my body into an uncomfortable bend. So much for trying to kick the tail light out I guess.

I was trying not to cry, but the panic was pushing tears into my eyes. He stood back for a moment as if admiring the scene before him, and to my absolute disgust, he'd taken out his phone to take a photo. "Just...perfect." He smiled, and my stomach clenched in fear as he closed the trunk, leaving me in darkness.

There was no way I could do anything with my phone right now, not unless the ghost of Harry Houdini chose this moment to possess my body. But it should still be turned on, and as long as I had battery life, they could find me. Or at least, I had to hope they would. But if Everett was dead...

I shoved the thought down. No, if Everett was hurt, then Jaime would call someone else, maybe Sergeant Jeffreys! Yes, he would tell the police, and the police would come looking for me. I just had to be alive when they finally got here. And I could do that, I could play along with this guy's sick little fantasy long enough for the cavalry to catch up to us. He thought he was rescuing me, so he wouldn't be planning to hurt me...right?

Every time the car slowed to a stop my whole body tensed in fear, waiting for the trunk to open at any moment. It felt like we had been driving for hours, my arms were asleep and my back was starting to twinge painfully with every bump we went over. My eyelids were starting to grow heavy despite my terror, but I forced myself to stay awake - to stay alert.

Finally, the car stopped, and I heard the engine cut off. I stiffened, and after a moment the trunk lifted and my eyes, accustomed to the darkness, struggled to adjust to the light. I recoiled when a hand reached towards me, and I heard him chuckle as he pulled me towards him, cutting the rope connecting my arms and legs. I felt a brief surge of relief as the aching muscles in my lower back released, but it was quickly replaced by sinking dread as he picked me up and swung me over his shoulder.

"If you scream, I'll have to punish you." He told me quietly, patting the back of my calf. I fought the urge to kick him, but he needn't have worried, his shoulder pressing into my diaphragm was enough to keep me from letting out more than a wheeze as he carried me away from the car. We were in some sort of dingy apartment building parkade, and he strolled so casually into the elevator with me over his shoulder that you'd think he had done this before. Ugh...maybe he actually had done this before. I shivered with fear and disgust, hating that his hands were still on me. I willed someone - anyone - to see us, but the building seemed to be deserted. We made it up to the seventh floor, and all the way down the hallway to his apartment - 712 I noted, just in case - without even hearing another living soul. Just my luck, I guess.

Once we were inside the apartment, I heard him give a small sigh in relief, so maybe it was mostly luck that had gotten us up here unnoticed. He walked further inside and for one horrifying moment, I thought he was taking me into his bedroom. Instead, he set me down on the ancient couch, facing the window in the main room. I stayed quiet for a bit, watching as he busied himself around the apartment, locking the door, turning on a few lights, and grabbing a bottle out of the fridge.

"I got us champagne, I know how much you like it." He announced, and the pop of the cork made me flinch. I tried to sit up, but my arms were still tied behind my back, making it difficult to readjust on the squishy cushions. I managed to get into a half-seated position, leaning with my side on the arm of the couch, my legs curled up underneath me. My dress was riding up my thighs, but I wasn't exactly in a position to demand modesty at this moment. He came around the couch with two glasses, smiling like we were on our first date, looking not at all like someone who'd just kidnapped a stranger.

He really was...a ghost. At least, that felt like the best way to describe him. He was medium height, average build - although clearly stronger than he looked, judging by how easily he'd picked me up. His hair was a dull brown, cut short and not styled. Even his clothes were dull, jeans and a faded tee-shirt under a plain black jacket. He had no defining features, nothing you could point to and say something like *Oh ya, that guy! The one with the big scar*. He was completely and utterly forgettable, and I felt a small ounce of pity for him. Only a little though, he had shoved me in a fucking trunk after all.

I tried not to flinch as he settled down on his knees in front of me. "I'm so glad we're finally together." He breathed. "You don't know how long I've waited for this moment Katerina." I shuddered when he used my full name. No one but my mother did that, and even she knew how much it bothered me.

"You...never introduced yourself," I replied, forcing my voice to be calm. "What can I call you?" *Besides creep, asshole, evil fucking bastard...*

He looked at me, and for a moment I thought I had already fucked up and said the wrong thing. But then he barked out a laugh, and I let out a breath I didn't know I'd been holding. This whole situation was a terrifying tightrope act, and I was already losing my balance.

"Silly me, of course." He smiled. "You can call me Greg."

Chapter 22

Kacey

"Nice to...finally meet you, Greg." I swallowed nervously. "Do you think that maybe, we could untie my hands? For a toast?" I smiled sweetly, motioning to the glasses in his hand with my chin.

"Certainly!" Greg jumped to his feet, setting the glasses down on the table beside me. Then he fished a familiar-looking knife out of his jacket, and I didn't move an inch as he sat beside me, reaching behind my back. He cut the rope, freeing my hands, but made no move to untie my feet. He also set the knife down beside him where I could still see it - threat loud and clear. My hands might be free, but I was not going anywhere anytime soon. I sat up properly and flinched as he reached towards me, but his arms moved past to snag the glasses behind me.

"Cheers!" He proclaimed, handing me a glass. I took it, hand trembling, and touched my glass to his. He watched me until I took I sip, and then he took a sip of his own. I hardly tasted it as it slid down my throat, the bubbles having none of their usual cheering effect.

"You are so much more beautiful up close," Greg announced abruptly, and I forced a smile, feeling sick. His eyes roamed my body, making my skin crawl. Unlike the looks that Everett gave me, which filled me with intense heat, this felt more like an assessment, and I was terrified of what would happen if I came up short. "You shouldn't feel the need to wear such revealing clothes." His fingers skimmed the lace along my side, and I cringed away from his touch, gritting my teeth behind my smile. "But you won't have to wear this sort of thing anymore."

"Oh? And why is that?" I asked hesitantly, and he took another sip of his drink, grinning like the Cheshire Cat.

"Because I'm here to take care of you now," Greg replied as if it was the most obvious thing in the world. "Now drink up, we're celebrating!"

His gaze turned sharp, so I took another sip, and then another, until he finally softened once more. His mood shifted so suddenly between one breath to the next, that I didn't know how to act. I needed to give him what he wanted, at least until Everett - or whoever was coming for me - could get here, but he was completely unpredictable, it felt like anything might set him off.

"I'm glad you still like this brand, I know you haven't had it for a while. I also picked up your other favourites, so you'd feel more at home." My blood ran cold, and I shook so hard I almost dropped my glass.

"H-How do you know what I like?" I asked, trying to sound coy, but it came out more whiny than I'd wanted. He gave me an exasperated look like I was the dumb one for not knowing.

"I've been studying you of course. It's what a good boyfriend does." He pointed to the telescope propped in front of one of his windows. It was not pointed to the sky, as most telescopes were, but instead, it was pointed slightly lower down, aiming at the buildings nearby. "Once I found where you lived, I knew I had to stay close by to keep you safe. This place wasn't the nicest, but it gave me the perfect view to keep an eye on you." My stomach rolled, the glass shaking in my hand. I kept the smile plastered to my face, taking a small sip of champagne while I thought up a response better than *have you considered professional psychiatric help?!*

"How thoughtful." That was all I managed to choke out. He seemed content with that at least, and I exhaled with a shudder. I needed to think fast, maybe if I played along well enough, I could get him to drop his guard and make a mistake.

"I really appreciate your hospitality." I smiled wanly. "But, unfortunately, I do have to get back eventually - for work of course. I can still come visit obviously." I was starting to babble, and I tried to keep the hysteria I was feeling from creeping into my voice. I would not cry in front of him, I promised myself.

To my dismay, he didn't fall for it. Greg just laughed, patting my thigh absently. "No, you don't need to work anymore sweetheart." He smiled. "Now that we're together, you'll only take pictures for me." My lungs stuttered like he'd knocked the wind out of me. I needed to think fast and come up with a different angle.

"Of-of course," I mumbled, smiling as if he was doing me a favour. "Well then, I'll at least need to go home to get some of my things-"

"I have everything you need right here," Greg interjected sharply, his eyes taking on that hard glint. His fingers tightened on my thigh, and I trembled. This conversation felt like I was treading water, and my head was slipping underwater.

"You're right. I was being silly." I laughed lightly, trying to diffuse the moment. "You've thought of everything already, of course."

"Of course I have." Greg snapped, making me flinch. "It's all I've been thinking about for months, while you flit around to parties and post slutty pictures and date jerks who don't deserve to touch you!" He was raising his voice now, his hand gripping me so hard I knew it would leave a bruise. "I know you were just trying to make me jealous, but you shouldn't have let them put their hands on you. They were trash! How dare they get to touch what's mine!" I started to shake, unable to stop the terror that was spreading through my body. He must've felt it, because he stopped shouting and just gave a deep sigh, scooting closer until I was almost sitting in his lap.

"I'm...I'm sorry," I whispered, hating myself for saying those words. He didn't deserve a sorry, not after everything he'd done. But I needed to get out of here alive, so I'd tell him sorry a thousand times if it bought me the time I needed. Greg put his arm around me, gripping me possessively.

"I know you are. And you're here now, so that's all that matters." He smiled, the rage dissipating in a flash.

I needed to get the fuck out here. Thinking fast, I drained my glass of champagne and gave him my best sultry smile. "How about a refill?"

I asked, holding up my empty glass. His eyes lit up, and I saw a flash of hunger in them that made my stomach lurch.

"Sure thing sweetheart." He smiled, and slid out from under my legs, grabbing my glass. As soon as he rounded the corner I fished my phone out of my dress. I sent up a prayer for battery life - and when the screen lit up, a second prayer for at least one bar of service. Somehow I had both, so I was not out of luck just yet. I quickly pulled up Everett's contact and typed out a message.

apt712 - shitty old bldg view of condo windows

I hit send, watching the little bubble float off with my only hope left. Please let Everett be alive, and please let him see this message.

"What do you think you're doing Katerina?" My heart dropped, and I turned to see Greg beside me, champagne in hand. I think my luck just ran out.

Chapter 23

Everett

I was breaking all kinds of laws, going at least 30 over the posted limit as I sped down the empty streets of lower downtown. Thankfully it was late enough that there weren't a lot of other people on the road because I had ripped through at least four red lights, not even paying attention to the colour anymore. Jaime was rattling off directions in my ear, leading me to our final destination. The police were on their way as well, but it looked like I was going to beat them there by several minutes at least.

My heart was pounding in my chest, and my poor body felt like it had been run over by a garbage truck. Whatever drugs the stalker had given me were wearing off, but the hangover it left behind was something reminiscent of my old college beer pong tournaments. I couldn't stop thinking about Kacey in that photo. Was she scared? Did she know we were coming for her? That *I* was coming for her? I had failed her - my one job was to keep her safe, and I had fucked it up. I'd let him get the jump on me, and now she was gone. If he hurt her, if he put so much as a finger on her - I'd never forgive myself.

"Fuck!" I snarled, slamming my fist into the steering wheel. I swerved around a car, ignoring their honking behind me. I should slow down, I needed to actually survive long enough to make it to where he had her. Instead, I pressed my foot on the gas peddle, gunning it through another red light.

"-You doing okay boss?" Jaime piped up from my ear. The poor bastard had been working double-duty tonight, on top of me yelling in his ear, and I would need to give him a week off to make up for this nightmarish evening. If I was still around for that.

"I'm fine." I bit out. "Sorry man. Just...frustrated." I ran my hand through my hair, and I could feel it sticking up from all of the sweat and dried blood and whatever else I'd managed to get it in tonight. I really wanted a shower and some painkillers. But first I needed Kacey.

"I get it man." Jaime sighed in my ear. "And I'm sorry to do this to you, but I've got more frustrating news. The location services are too weak, her service is probably shit in these old concrete buildings. I can't pinpoint the exact one that they're in. I'll keep trying, but I've only been able to narrow it down to three buildings on one corner."

I swore in my head so Jaime wouldn't have to listen to another one of my profane tirades. It wasn't his fault anyway, he was doing the best he could, we just had shit luck. Three buildings...even if we had an army of cops, how could we search three buildings before he heard us and bolted...or worse? I couldn't think about the worst-case scenario right now, because that just wasn't an option. I would find her, and I would beat the ever-loving shit out of the asshole that took her. My hands clenched on the steering wheel, and I finally slowed as I rounded the corner onto yet another nearly empty street. I could see what must've been the three buildings, only a few blocks away now. They were clustered together like an ominous puzzle - if only he had a neon flashing STALKER sign hanging on his window, now that would've been considerate.

Police hadn't arrived yet, and the street was eerily quiet. I pulled up on the curb to watch the buildings, looking for any signs of life, studying the conundrum in front of me. Somewhere close by, Kacey was in mortal danger, and all I could do was sit here like a jackass and wait for a miracle to fall into my lap.

My phone buzzed in my pocket, and I thought about ignoring it but decided to check, just in case the perp had posted something new. My heart jumped into my throat, seeing a new text from Kacey.

"Jaime she sent a text," I told him, in complete disbelief. My hands shook as I opened the message.

apt712 - shitty old bldg view of condo windows

That's my girl! "Apartment 712, an old building with a view of condo windows? Her condo probably." I told Jaime quickly. "Does that narrow it down?"

I could hear Jaime typing through my earpiece, and I waited impatiently, studying the buildings in front of me. He suddenly gave a whoop of celebration.

"Fuck yes, it does!" He shouted, and it was my turn to wince at the volume. "One of the buildings is an empty warehouse, the other is only five stories. That leaves only one that she could be in." He rattled off the address, which turned out to be the one I'd parked nearest to. I got out of my car and pulled out my gun, clicking the safety off.

"Let Sergeant Jeffreys know to go to apartment 712," I told him, crossing the street, gun at my side. "Tell him I'm going in."

I'm coming for you Kacey, just hold on a little longer.

Chapter 24

Kacey

"I was just shutting down my accounts." I lied quickly as Greg rounded the sofa. He set the glasses down on the table and grabbed my phone out of my hand. He unlocked it - because of course, he had my password. My heart sank as the messages opened, showing him what I'd sent to Everett.

"You texted him?!" He shouted, throwing my phone at the wall, and shattering it to pieces. I flinched, shrinking back into the couch away from him, my hands up in supplication. "Why the fuck would you text that disgusting piece of shit!" he snarled. He looked rabid, his eyes wide and manic, his face morphed into something close to inhumane.

"If-If he knows where I am, he won't have to come looking for me." I babbled, searching for a way to save this, or at least stall for time. My brain felt like it was short-circuiting, fear making the words tumble from my mouth. "So I can stay here, w-with you."

"Liar!" He screamed, lunging forward. He grabbed my legs and pulled me roughly off the couch. I landed flat on my back, smacking my head against the floor. I couldn't breathe for a moment, my lungs seizing, and I just gaped up at him in terror.

"I told you I would have to punish you if you didn't behave." Greg hissed, and knelt down on top of me, pinning me to the floor. He grabbed his knife off the couch and looked down at me with a sigh. Oh god, he was actually going to kill me.

"You'll learn to love me, Katerina, I promise. But you have to be obedient." On the last word, he slammed the knife into the floor beside my face, the blade digging into the hardwood. A whimper escaped my lips. "I don't want to hurt you, but it's the only way you'll learn."

With my last remaining scrap of strength, I screamed at him and scratched at his face and neck with my nails. He swore loudly and grabbed for my hands, and we fought like that for a few desperate moments until he finally caught both my wrists, pinning them above my head with his hand. I had gotten him good on his cheek at least, and fresh blood welled up in the deep grooves I'd left in his face.

His eyes were dark as he glared at me, his teeth bared in an inhumane snarl, and then he wrapped his hand around my throat and began to squeeze. I jerked and twisted my body desperately, trying to knock him off of me or get one of my hands free, but his grip was like cold steel. He stared at me, unblinking, and I stared back defiantly, blackness already creeping in around the edges of my vision as my brain screamed out for oxygen. I stopped struggling as everything started to fade out, my energy spent. Just then, the hand on my neck loosened enough for air to slip in, and gasped in a breath, my chest heaving.

Greg smiled cruelly, squeezing his hand again until I started thrashing, tears finally escaping and running hot down my cheek. This time I think I did lose consciousness for a few moments, until he loosened his grip once again. He laughed as I gasped for air, my singular focus to get oxygen back into my lungs. I let out a sob, pain radiating down my throat.

His hand moved up from my throat to grasp my chin, fingers digging painfully into my skin. "Are you going to misbehave again?" He demanded, eyes flashing.

"N-no." I whimpered hoarsely, and more tears rolled down my cheeks. I was still trying to catch my breath, but my throat felt tight like his hand was still squeezing it.

"Good. Now, how about you apologize and start making it up to me?" He mused, trailing his hand back down my neck, towards my chest.

A noise from outside made him pause and look up, and he frowned in confusion. It was like a small explosion went off, something slamming into the door with a horrible bang. Greg leapt up, and for a brief, blissful moment I was free of his weight. Using the momentary distraction, I started crawling towards the door. It wasn't an easy feat when my ankles were still bound, and he caught me before I could get far. He grabbed a handful of my hair and wrenched me backwards, and I cried out in pain as he lifted me back up into his arms.

From this position at least I could watch as the door shuddered one last time before it gave in, exploding open with a crash. I couldn't make out who it was as bits of the doorframe scattered across the apartment and drywall dust rained from the ceiling, obscuring the doorway. Greg shoved the knife back up against my throat, gripping me tightly as he pulled us backwards away from the debris.

Relief flooded through me when Everett stepped over the wreckage of the door, his gun levelled at Greg. A small sob escaped my lips, happiness bubbling up in my chest even as Greg's knife pricked my already damaged neck. He was alive, and he had found me, just like I knew he would.

"Stop right there! One more step and I'll kill her, I swear I will!" Greg yelled, yanking me back against him. The knife was pressing into me so hard now I could feel blood running down my neck. The sharp sting of the blade added to the already suffocating tightness I felt in my throat, the pain starting to make me woozy. Or maybe it was the lack of oxygen that was doing that.

It felt like the whole world slowed down in that moment, stretching time out like taffy. My heartbeat pounded in my ears, muffling Greg's shouts. Everett looked into my eyes, steadying me, bolstering my strength just as my legs threatened to give out. Then he dropped his gaze to my neck, where I could feel the bruises from my 'punishment' already forming even as Greg's knife bit into my skin. A look passed over Everett's face that I had never seen before, something so cold and calculating that the hairs on my arms stood up. It disappeared in a flash, replaced by deadly determination, and I watched his jaw set as he made his decision clear.

Oh god, this wasn't going to be pretty. He met my eyes and gave me a small nod. I tipped my head in response, wary of too much movement because of the knife. I closed my eyes tight, my pulse racing.

A millisecond later I heard two loud pops, and the world sped up back to normal. Pain streaked across my neck as the weight pressing against me fell away. My eyes flew open, and I saw the knife on the ground, still clutched in Greg's hand. Greg was sprawled across the floor behind me, eyes wide and unseeing, mouth still open from the tirade he'd been spewing. Even with two bullet holes in his face, he still looked completely unremarkable, just a pathetic, dead ghost.

I don't know how long I stood over his body, frozen in place, until I felt a tug around my ankles, and watched the rope that was still tied around my legs slip off, landing on the floor beside Greg. Then someone was grabbing me, pressing something against my neck.

"Kace, baby are you okay? Can you hear me?" Everett's hand gripped my shoulder, tugging me away from where my legs had taken root in Greg's dingy living room. I shivered and wrapped my arms around my chest, my hands encountering dampness along my skin. I pulled my hand up to see blood, now smeared along my arm. Greg's blood? Or mine? I wasn't sure. I felt something warm envelop my shoulders, making me flinch. But it was only a jacket - Everett's suit jacket - that was being draped over me. It was warm and smelled like him, and I pulled it tighter around myself, finally able to look at him again.

"I thought you were dead," I told him, my voice barely a rasp thanks to my injuries. He pulled me against his chest, and I could feel his warmth sinking into my tired body. The building started to shake, or maybe it was just me, it was hard to tell anymore. A sob tumbled from my lips, and then another, and soon a cascade of tears fell down my face as all of my pain and fear bubbled up to the surface. My legs finally gave out, and Everett scooped me up into his arms, holding me tightly as I pressed my face against his chest, soaking his shirt with my tears.

I felt us moving, and other voices floated in around us, but I was crying too hard to make out what they were saying.

"She needs a doctor, she's in shock and bleeding badly." I heard Everett say, and I wondered briefly who had been hurt. We were moving again, and I closed my eyes, exhaustion slowly replacing the tears. Everett would get me home now, it was safe to finally sleep.

Chapter 25

Everett

"Kacey, keep your eyes open for me okay?" I begged her, shaking her gently as I held her in my arms. I saw her eyes blink open slowly, but they were unfocused, and I wasn't sure if she was even hearing me at this point. "Come on Kace, just a little longer, please! We're almost at the ambulance." I broke into a run once the elevator doors opened, and the EMTs waiting in the lobby jumped into action as I approached. I set Kacey on the stretcher, her eyes fluttering open again briefly to meet mine. She mouthed something at me, but I didn't catch the words, her voice barely a rasp. Her lips were tinged blue like she wasn't getting enough air. The EMTs worked quickly to strap in her, moving her outside and into the awaiting ambulance. I hopped inside after them, and we sped off towards the hospital, siren blaring.

"She's got a deep gash on her neck from a knife," I told them as one of the EMTs pulled off the towel I'd wrapped over her wound. It was still oozing blood, and he quickly replaced it with some fresh towels. "There's other damage too, bruising around her throat. She can't talk very well. I think she's in shock." I watched helplessly as he started to attach wires to her hand and chest, flipping on the monitors beside her. I watched her heart rate blip across the screen, a little too slow for my liking.

"I'm starting an IV, she's lost a lot of blood." He told me, and I grabbed Kacey's free hand, giving it a gentle squeeze. She looked so pale, her eyes barely opening after each blink. "Come on Ms. Keeper, stay awake for us okay? We're almost at the hospital now." The EMT pressed an oxygen mask over her mouth, and she took a deep, shaky breath. "She's definitely got damage to her throat, I can't tell if it's just swelling or something more, we'll need a CT to confirm." He told me, checking on the cut once more. The bleeding seemed to have slowed, was that good or bad?

We screeched to a stop in front of the hospital doors, and the EMT handed Kacey off to a group of nurses who wheeled us inside. I held her hand as they pushed her stretcher down the hall. Her eyes weren't open anymore, and the monitors attached to her were beeping angrily.

"Nobody past this point." One of the nurses said abruptly putting a hand on my chest. I let go of Kacey's hand and they continued past me, through a set of doors.

"Can't I stay with her, please?" I asked her desperately. I just got her back, I couldn't lose her again so soon.

"Not in there I'm afraid." She told me firmly. "Someone will come and update you as soon as possible. Just wait here for now, okay?" She pointed behind me to the half-empty waiting room. Before I could argue further, she disappeared behind the doors.

Dejected, I sat down in one of the seats facing the doors and dropped my head into my hands. I must have been a sight - covered in blood, my shirt rumpled and damp from Kacey's tears. I'd given my gun to one of the officers at the scene so they could match it to the bullets they'd be pulling out of Greg. I sent a message to Jaime, and then another to Alexis, letting them know that Kacey was safe and at the hospital. My job was done - Now all I could do was wait.

The events of the night replayed in my mind over and over, as I analyzed every move I'd made. I'd honestly had no idea what I was going to find when I finally reached the apartment. I had heard noises on the other side of the door that sounded like a struggle and hadn't bothered waiting for the police to show up. I kicked the door in viciously and stormed in with my gun drawn, searching for the bastard. My first feeling had been visceral relief, seeing Kacey alive and standing. Unfortunately, the coward had been quick, and he had Kacey propped up in front of him like a human shield, blocking my shot.

He had started shouting at me immediately, threatening to kill her if I came any closer. He had looked out of his mind, spit flying from his mouth as he screamed at me, and I knew there would be no negotiations. There was no way to reason with someone as completely disconnected from reality as he was. I had seen the fear in Kacey's eyes, blood already running down her neck from the knife digging into her throat. I knew he wouldn't let her leave this apartment, and I needed to act quickly before he hurt her any more than he already had. I had given Kacey a little nod, so subtle he wouldn't have noticed, still spewing a tirade of rage and insanity towards me. She had somehow seemed to understand what I meant to do, and her head had moved ever so slightly to the side, just enough to give me a clear shot.

I hadn't planned on killing him, honestly, but he'd left me no other choice. I felt no remorse when I shot him once, then twice for good measure. The first shot had killed him instantly, and he'd dropped to the floor with a terrible thud, leaving Kacey in the middle of the room with her eyes clamped shut. The risk I took had been calculated - I knew I could make the shot from that distance without hitting her, but I wasn't sure about what would happen with his hand, and the knife he had to her throat. The risk was high, but there was no time to figure out a better plan, so I decided to worry about the collateral damage after I took care of the problem at hand. Once he'd hit the ground, I'd grabbed a tea towel off the nearby countertop and ran to Kacey, pressing it against her neck to try to staunch the bleeding. The knife had sliced down as he had fallen, but the cut was shallow, missing any major arteries. She had started shivering, her eyes wide but oddly vacant - probably from shock, so I'd given her my jacket. It was definitely a little worse for wear, but she didn't seem to mind it.

"I thought you were dead." That was all she'd said, and my heart ached. She hadn't known I was alive, and yet, she'd still texted me and not anyone else. Because even in death I would've found a way to get to her.

I'd pulled her tightly to my chest as she started to cry, wishing that I could absorb her pain as my own. When her knees had buckled, I finally jolted back into action, scooping her up into my arms. The police had started to arrive, taking in the scene before them. Sergeant Jefferys was there, I was mildly impressed that he's actually showed up in person for this. Kacey's parents must've been extremely important people to warrant his undivided attention.

I'd handed him my gun directly, not wanting it to get lost among the sea of cops now swarming us. It needed to be taken into evidence, but I liked my gun, and I wanted it back eventually. "I need a statement and your version of events." He had told me cooly, and I knew I was going to get a tongue-lashing for not waiting for the actual officers to arrive.

"She needs a doctor, she's in shock and bleeding badly. I'll be at the hospital, you can take my statement there." I replied evenly and brushed past him. To his credit, he hadn't stopped me, and neither did anyone else I passed on the way down to the ambulance.

Chapter 26

Everett

I waited for hours in that tiny waiting room, stuffed into a chair that was altogether too small for a guy my size. At some point, night had turned into morning, and the bustle of people grew louder around me as the day began. I stared holes in the door, waiting for someone to come out with news. Every time it opened I perked up, only to be disappointed when they went over to someone else. My eyes felt like they were coated in a layer of sand, and every part of my body was aching from everything I'd put it through in the last week. I needed a vacation - or a quieter job. I could work at a library, or be a personal trainer - that might be fun.

I think the lack of sleep was starting to get to me.

"Everett!" Someone shouted, making me jump out of my seat. I turned to see Layla running down the hall towards me, earning a glare from a passing nurse. Her hair was half up in a bun, and she was wearing a large hoodie and raggedy pyjama pants with crocs. She must've been in bed when Alexis called her with news about Kacey and drove right over. To my complete surprise, she didn't slow down and instead tackled me, wrapping her arms around my chest. I hugged her back awkwardly, caught off guard by her reaction.

"You killed him right?" Layla asked, her eyes shining with pure, unadulterated rage. If I said no, I had a feeling she would've finished the job herself.

"He's dead," I told her quietly - and I wouldn't lose any sleep over it either. She gave a curt nod and wiped her eyes brusquely before storming off to the nearby nurse's station, probably to interrogate someone on Kacey's status. I sat - or rather collapsed - back into my chair, resuming my door-watching duties. I closed my eyes for just a moment to try and coax some moisture into them, and suddenly

Layla had reappeared, sitting down beside me holding two large cups. I must've drifted off for a few minutes.

"Coffee." She announced, holding out one of the cups, which I took gratefully. "You look like shit." She told me, not unkindly, slumping down in her own seat and taking a long drink. I took a sip of my own, wondering how it was possible that even now Layla still had this effortless grace about her. Maybe she was a witch.

Fuck, I really needed to sleep.

We drank our coffee in silence, and I felt a little sliver of life return to my body as the warm caffeine entered my bloodstream. To my dismay, it faded quickly, unable to fight against the weight of the exhaustion in my bones.

Finally, just as I'd begun to nod off again, someone in a white coat walked out, zeroing in on me. I stood up quickly and cleared my throat, Layla jumping up to join me.

"Mr. Keeper?" She asked, and I was confused for a moment before remembering that Kacey had still been wearing her fake engagement ring.

"No, I'm Cole. Uh, Everett Cole, sorry." The caffeine and the sleep deprivation were duking it out in my brain, making basic functions like speech significantly harder. "Kace- Katerina Keeper is my fiancé." It didn't matter if it wasn't technically real, at this point I'd tell them we were married if it meant I could see her sooner.

"Alright, then Mr...Cole." The doctor smiled kindly. "I'm Dr. Schefield. Kacey has been moved to a bed in the ICU for now. The cut on her throat was clean and relatively shallow, missing her big arteries. We have her on an IV with some antibiotics to prevent infection and fluids because she lost a lot of blood and her blood pressure is not where I'd like it. The plastic surgeon is just finishing stitching her up now, and he assured me that the scarring would be quite minimal."

I clenched my fists at my side, relief flooding through my tired body. "So, she's okay then, right? She'll be okay?"

"Our pressing concern at the moment is the blunt trauma to her throat. I ordered a chest and head CT, which revealed significant laryngeal trauma." Dr. Schefield explained, and I tried my best to keep up. "Now, the good news is we did not find any evidence of edema, fractures or laryngeal rupture. The bad news is that she will need to stay here in the hospital until her O2 stats improve, a few days at least. But she will need to rest even after she is released, for a couple of weeks at least, eating only liquidy foods like broth, and ice cream, and minimal speaking to avoid any additional strain on her vocal cords."

I nodded along and saw Layla taking vigorous notes on her phone. "When can we see her?" I asked anxiously. I heard what she was saying, but some part of me needed to see her and confirm with my own eyes that she was safe and whole.

"She's resting now, and she needs the sleep. But if you want to go sit with her *quietly* -" she emphasized, with a stern look and each of us. "I will have the nurse show you to her room. I've also let the police know that she is not to be bothered until tomorrow at the earliest."

"Thank you, doctor, I really appreciate it. We'll be quiet I promise." I assured her. She gave me a small smile and waved a nurse over.

We followed the nurse through a different set of doors, these ones leading to the ICU. Kacey was in a private little room, and I'm sure it had something to do with her last name. How rich were her parents exactly?

Kacey looked tiny in the bed, propped up on a small mountain of pillows so she was almost sitting up. An IV was hooked up, dripping quietly along with the steady beat of her heart rate on the monitor. She had tubing running to her face, pumping oxygen into her nose. Bandages covered some of her neck, but the rest that was showing was already turning a horrible purple. Her eyes were closed, and as promised, Layla and I crept in and each took up a chair on either side of the bed, careful not to wake her.

I leaned forward, resting my arms carefully on the bed so I could hold Kacey's hand. "I'm sorry I didn't get there sooner," I whispered, pressing my forehead against her hand. If Layla heard me, she pretended she hadn't, busy typing into her phone.

We sat vigil together for a while until I nodded off, still holding Kacey's hand, my head resting on the bed. I was only vaguely aware when Layla got up, and I felt her touch my arm when she whispered "I'll be back later, text me if she wakes up." I'm not sure how long I slept, my body was finally able to relax now that she was safe and at my side.

Chapter 27

Kacey

I woke up in an unfamiliar bed, which was both confusing and terrifying, especially given all that had happened this week. Everything ached, from my toes up to my scalp, and my throat spasmed horribly every time I tried to swallow. Memories started to bleed back into my brain - Everett on the ground, unmoving - the trunk - Greg's hand on my throat. Something behind me started beeping like crazy, and I struggled to breathe, every inhale felt like I was sucking air through a straw, and every exhale was a wheeze. Someone squeezed my hand, and I finally noticed the hulking figure resting on the bed beside me.

"Kacey, it's me, Everett, you're okay." He picked up my hand in his, kissing it tenderly. "You're safe, you're at the hospital." His words bounced around in my head for a moment before sinking in, and I wheezed a sigh of relief, the beeping above my head slowing.

"I-" I tried to say something, but my throat constricted around the words, setting off a fit of coughing. Everett hurriedly pressed a button on my bed, looking around the room. A nurse came in, moving to my side immediately, Everett clearing out of her way.

"I think she needs water." He told her, and she checked my IV and the tubing around my face. I nodded, wincing, I would like some water.

"Sure thing hon." She replied and was out the door quickly as a flash.

"Don't try to talk yet, okay?" Everett told me, right back at my side. "Your throat was damaged, it needs to rest so it can heal." *Bad news for you, eh?* Why was it that I only had clever retorts when no one would be able to hear them?

The nurse returned with a pitcher and a small plastic cup with a straw. "Drink slowly, little sips only." She instructed me, handing me the cup. I took a small sip, and my throat spasmed again as I swallowed, but it eased the burning somewhat. Satisfied that I could manage a cup of water without dying, the nurse turned and left. I tried a couple more sips, but somehow even the effort of drinking was exhausting, so I set the cup down on a nearby tray to take a break.

Everett was hovering by my side, and he looked about as good as I felt. The dark circle under his good eye matched the horrible purple bruise on the other half of his face, and there was dry blood smeared across his forehead, his eyebrow now looking swollen and decidedly less healed than it had before the party. Now instead of mysterious, he looked positively ghoulish in the unflattering hospital light. I had so many questions for him, and no way to ask, which pissed me off more than anything.

"W-" I tried again, letting out a frustrated wheeze when the word stuck in my throat.

"No talking." He frowned at me. I lifted up my hands in a -*well what then?* - gesture, glaring at him. He looked around for a moment, then tugged his phone out of his pocket. Where was my phone again? Oh right. I winced, remembering how it had smashed when it hit the wall. I guess I'd be needing a new one after all.

"Here, use this." He smiled and handed me his phone, already open to the notes app. He took a seat while I began typing furiously. I handed it back to him after a minute, and he looked down the list I'd made.

How long have I been here? "You've been here close to 24 hours." He told me softly. "I brought you here last night, it was pretty late. You got some scans and they stitched you up, and you've been sleeping ever since."

What happened to you? "What happened at the dinner? My best guess is that he stuck me with something when he bumped into me earlier that night. It knocked me out for an hour or so." Everett rubbed a hand over his face, looking pained. I patted his arm gently, trying to convey through touch how much it was not his fault. Everett took my hand in his, giving it a gentle squeeze before turning back to my list of questions.

Is he really dead? "Yes, he's dead, I made sure of it." He told me, his jaw clenching. I nodded dully, remembering Greg's body on the floor, seeing the holes in his face that weren't supposed to be there. He was really gone -and unless he was truly a ghost, he wouldn't be able to haunt me anymore.

When can I get out of here? My last question. Everett paused for a moment, chewing the inside of his cheek. "I'm not sure on this one, the doctor said you'd need to be here for a couple of days at least until you're breathing well enough again." I looked down at my lap, a tear escaping and rolling down my cheek. I just wanted to go home - although my condo didn't feel much like home anymore. Knowing that he'd been watching me for weeks, or months even like I was an animal in a zoo, made me sick to my stomach.

I reached for his phone back, annoyed by this slow process already. I typed quickly, then took another careful sip of water while he read it.

He was watching me in my condo with a telescope, he could see everything I did. Everett looked like he might break his phone, and I slipped it gently out of his clenched hands before he snapped my last method of communication.

"Don't worry, we can fix it." He told me, eyes blazing with rage. "There's a coating you can get that can turn your windows into a sort of one-way mirror, so you can see out but people can't see in. I can install some for you, it should only take a day or two at most. Or, you can move. I know a couple of guys, we can have your stuff packed up in no time. Don't worry about your lease, I'll deal with that. When it's a matter of personal security it's easy enough to negotiate. I bet we could even have Sergeant Jeffreys put in a word for you, I can call him later if you like, and find out what your options are."

I couldn't help but smile, watching him jump into problem-solving mode. This was exactly what he'd needed, a problem that he could solve. He couldn't fix my broken throat, but he could figure out a way to get me out of a lease. I let him continue rambling, his voice washing over me with a reassuring normalcy that eased the tension in my chest. I didn't know yet if I wanted to move, or if I'd stay and try and make the best of it. But I didn't need to figure that out right away.

Someone knocked, and a woman in a white coat walked into the room, halting Everett's detailed moving plans. "I'm glad to see you awake." She smiled, grabbing my chart off the wall. "You probably don't remember meeting me earlier, I'm Dr. Schefield." I watched her review the papers briefly before returning the chart to it's place beside the door. She was right, I had no memory of seeing her before. The last several hours of my life were a complete blank in my memory, but that was probably for the best anyway.

"I wanted to review a couple of things with you now that you've had some time to rest - just yes and no questions for today, is that alright with you?" I nodded yes, and she smiled reassuringly, pulling a small notepad and a pen out of her coat pocket. "Wonderful."

"I'll give you some privacy," Everett announced, moving to stand. I grabbed his hand and shook my head, motioning for him to stay. He looked at Dr. Schefield to confirm, then sat back down, keeping his hand on the bed under mine. I didn't want him to leave, he made me feel safer when he was in the room. I knew the doctor wasn't about to stab me with her pen, but my nerves were shot and I was so tired, I just needed his hand to hold to keep me tethered to the earth.

"The police want to come by and get your statement as soon as possible. Are you comfortable meeting with them tomorrow morning?" She asked. I got the feeling that if I said no, she would bar the door herself to keep them away. I nodded, it would be better to get it over with anyway. I wasn't going to be able to give them much verbally, but I'm sure a written statement would work just fine given the circumstances.

"Okay." She nodded, making a little note on her notepad. Now, when you were brought in, we did a preliminary assessment to ensure that you didn't have any other dislocations or breaks that needed addressing." Her gaze shifted briefly to Everett, then back to me. "I did not order an internal exam at that time, because you weren't in a state to consent to that. But I can now, if you believe one is necessary and would like it included in the police report." I felt Everett grow very still next to me, and my stomach clenched. I shook my head, meeting her gaze evenly.

"We can still do the exam, even if you do not want it included in the police report." She told me carefully. "I just want to be certain that no injury is being left untreated." Oh for fucks sake, what I wouldn't give to be able to talk right now. I lifted my hands up, dropping Everett's in the process, and brushed off my very rusty charade skills. Motioning to my lower half, I shook my head, the same with my upper half. Then I pointed to my neck and nodded. Then, for honesty's sake, I pointed to my head and nodded again.

It felt like the air rushed back into the room all at once. Dr. Schefield smiled, with what was quite possibly relief in her eyes. "Very good then. We already retrieved some DNA from under your fingernails which was sent to their lab for processing, so that should be plenty for the police report." Damn right, they did. I would've taken his eyes out if I'd gotten the chance. "I'll be back tomorrow to check on you again, but I think we can get you out of here soon." She turned, leaving Everett and me alone in the room once more.

Everett appeared to be studying something quite fascinating in the far corner of the room, his eyes shining. He cleared his throat roughly, "I think that was a good sign." He told me, "Maybe you can leave earlier than we thought." He looked so damn tired, my heart ached. I gestured for him to come closer, and at once he was all concern. "What's wrong? Does something hurt? I can call her back if you want." I rolled my eyes and gestured again. He leaned forward, frowning, and I patted his cheek, feeling a hint of scratchy stubble beginning to form. Gently, as if he was afraid I would shatter on contact, he pressed his forehead against mine, closing his eyes.

"You were supposed to text me!" Layla snapped, scaring the shit out of both of us. Everett had the good sense to look afraid - I would be too, you did not want to get on Layla's bad side. She walked inside, oblivious to the moment she'd just stepped into. Her arms were full of bags, flowers and even a couple of balloons that told me to *Get Well Soon* with a big happy face. She dumped all of it haphazardly in a chair and nearly jumped on the bed, hugging me awkwardly to avoid the various bandages and tubes that covered my body. I gave her a reassuring squeeze, reminding her that I was, in fact, alive and well. Well, at least for the most part.

"I'll forgive you this once. But only because you're exhausted and look like a train wreck." She told Everett, and I smacked her on the arm. "What? It's true! He hasn't left since you were brought in. That's what that smell is you know." Everett laughed, and I whacked Layla again, giving her a sharp look. We'd both been through hell, and I'm sure I wasn't looking my best either. My hair was a tangled mess and my skin felt oily, I'm sure the makeup I'd had on before the event was still smeared all over my face since I doubted the ER doctors would take the time to remove it. I would give anything for a hot bath right now, but I doubt the hospital would accommodate that.

"I would've gone home and showered, honestly, but my car's not here." Everett shrugged. "It's probably still parked on the street, I'll see if Meagan can pick me up later." He stifled a yawn.

Layla rifled through her purse and grabbed her keys, which she tossed over the bed to him. "Here, just use mine. Go home, take a shower and have a nap. I'll cover the next shift." She smiled. Wow, she really must like Everett, even *I* wasn't allowed to drive her car.

Everett looked at her keys, then at me, clearly torn. I nodded emphatically and plugged my nose at him. "Alright, I get it! I'll take a shower." He smiled throwing his hands up in defeat, and I wheezed out a breath that was supposed to be a laugh.

He gave me a light kiss on the forehead, lingering just long enough for Layla to clear her throat loudly. "It's just a shower Casanova, not a trip to Guam." She teased. I aimed another smack, but she dodged this one.

"Be back soon," Everett whispered in my ear before walking out of the room. I watched Everett leave, smiling when he looked back at me once before disappearing around the corner. I wished I could go with him, I had no idea how I was going to handle being stuck in this room for another few hours, let alone a few days.

"Alright, since you're insisting on a new career as a mime, I brought a few supplies to make things easier." She dug through one of the bags she'd brought. "Ta-dah!" Layla produced a whiteboard and some dry-erase markers.

I needed to get my voice back soon, or I was going to lose my mind.

Chapter 28

Kacey

Layla had thought of everything, and along with the whiteboard, she'd also pulled out a hair brush and some face wipes. Together, the two of us managed to make me look a little less bedraggled. I still needed a shower, and a few day's worth of sleep wouldn't hurt, but at least now from the chin up I barely looked like I'd just survived a near-death experience. Layla stayed with me while I ate - or rather sipped - my dinner, and we scrolled through social media together for a few hours until I started to nod off.

When I woke up again, it must've been late, judging from the lack of light coming in from the window in my room. I looked over to where Layla had been sitting, but she'd been replaced by a familiar hulking form. Everett must've snuck in while I'd been asleep and done the shift hand-off with Layla. He looked a little better now that he had showered, and I noticed a fresh bandage on his eyebrow. He was dozing currently, his head tilted back, too big for the chair he was trying to sleep in. It was a superpower, being able to sleep anywhere you wanted at any time. He'd probably learned that trick when he'd been in the Marines. I felt myself relax now that he was back with me, and I settled myself once more into my pile of pillows. Sleep found me quickly, my body obviously still desperate for the rest it needed to heal.

The next two days passed in a dull blur of liquid meals, doctor's exams and mind-numbing boredom. The police finally came and got my written statement about how events had unfolded at Greg's apartment. I had to be very detailed in their report since someone had ended up dead. Reliving that horrible night all over again had me gasping for air, my throat clenching shut like Greg's hand was squeezing it all over again. Dr. Schefield ended up intervening midway through their questions, giving me something to calm the hysteria that built up in my chest whenever I thought about Greg kneeling over me with his knife. I fell asleep shortly after the police left that morning and spent the rest of the day in a blissful drug-induced unconsciousness.

Thanks to the medication, I was able to catch up on my sleep and then some. Now that I was rested, my frustration grew as my body refused to heal as fast as I would've liked. My throat still spasmed whenever I tried to drink more than a small sip at a time, and it would start to tighten if I tried to complete even the smallest of tasks. Any amount of exertion, even simply getting up to walk to the bathroom, felt like I was trying to run up the side of a cliff. The worst would be the panic that followed, my brain convinced that every time my throat constricted I was being strangled all over again. It was beginning to feel like I was at war with my own body.

I was mercifully discharged from the hospital on the third day, having improved my oxygen levels enough that I no longer needed the tank to breathe. There were several conditions to my release, however. which Dr. Schefield made abundantly clear. I needed a full-time babysitter around 24/7 for the first week I was at home since I was not allowed to do anything for myself. I also wasn't allowed to fall asleep with any less than 3 pillows propping me up, because laying down might cause my weakened throat to collapse and suffocate me in my sleep. I was also on a liquid diet - although when ice cream and jello became classified as liquids is beyond me. I couldn't lift anything heavy, talk above a whisper, or do anything that made me out of breath.

Talk about a lame week.

I still hadn't decided what to do about my condo, all I did know was that currently, I did not feel safe going back there. Everett, with an abundance of generosity - or possibly guilt - offered to let me stay at his place for a few days, since he'd already decided to become my bodyguard-turned-babysitter for the week. Layla brought a bag of my clothes to the hospital since all I had was a hospital gown and a blood-stained dress that I had every intention of shoving in the first garbage bin I saw. Those clothes would last me several days at least, so we wouldn't even need to stop by my condo for supplies.

I was so relieved to get outside again, the cool air fresh and crisp compared to the stale hospital air conditioning. Everett had coordinated with Meagan to retrieve his car the day before, which had somehow not been towed yet after sitting abandoned on the street for three days. The ride to his place was short and nearly silent, but in a peaceful sort of way. Everett clearly had a lot on his mind, his brow furrowed as he stared at the road. Maybe he was already regretting his offer to let me stay. I mean, did he even have enough room for someone to stay over? I was becoming more and more curious to see what sort of bachelor pad Everett lived in. Was he one of those guys with two pieces of furniture, one set of dishes and a single towel? Or maybe he the kind of guy who kept women's products in the bathroom for all the one-night stands he brought home.

Yikes, I think I would actually prefer the former.

His apartment building did not have a doorman, and it was definitely older but otherwise well-maintained. I approached the door with trepidation, anxious about what I'd find thanks to my overactive imagination. I was pleasantly surprised when I walked inside and discovered that Everett's home was perfectly ordinary, especially for a single bachelor. For one thing, it was completely furnished. There was a dining room table, complete with chairs, and the living room had a couch and a lounger set. There was even a throw blanket arranged on the back of the couch. I don't think I'd ever seen a throw blanket in a straight man's home before today, at least not if they were single. And while I wouldn't describe it as exactly sterile, he definitely cleaned up more than I did. There was hardly anything that I could describe as clutter on any visible surface. The apartment had a decent-sized kitchen and living room space, leading to a bathroom and a single bedroom at the end of the hall. He had a little desk area in the corner of the living room with a workspace set up, similar to what he'd rigged at my place.

Everett carried my bags to his room, leaving me to snoop around the living room. I wandered over to study the pictures on his wall, recognizing Meagan in a few of them. I saw a couple of Everett when he was younger, dressed in some sort of military uniform. He looked so severe with his hair cropped short, eyes staring off at something beyond the camera. My eyes were drawn to a clearly more recent photo, judging from his hairstyle. The photo showed Everett cozied up with someone I hadn't seen before.

I gestured him over impatiently when he emerged from the bedroom. "Who's this?" I demanded with a whisper, still not able to gather much volume with my words. He had the good sense to look guilty, rubbing his hand on his cheek.

"I know, I should've told you about her sooner, I just didn't know how to bring it up." Everett sighed, running a hand through his hair. What had he been thinking, keeping something like this from me? Had he hoped that I would just never find out?

"I can't believe you didn't tell me! Where is she?" If I could have yelled, I would've. We both turned when the door knob wiggled, and the door to his apartment swung open, hitting the wall with a bang.

A tiny black and white missile shot threw the door, slamming into Everett's chest, hard enough to knock him back a few steps. He laughed and spun around, holding what appeared to be a fuzzy blur in his arms. Meagan appeared shortly after, leash in hand.

"Hey, Kacey." She smiled. "I heard you guys get in. I live upstairs." She told me smugly, pointing up at the ceiling. "Sadie goes apeshit when she knows he's home, so I figured I'd drop her off."

"Kacey, this is my best girl, Sadie," Everett announced. The blur had calmed down enough to be visible to the human eye once more, content now to settle in Everett's arms and lick his face.

"She's gorgeous." I rasped, drawing her attention. She must be a border collie I surmised, based on my passing knowledge of dog breeds. She had one blue eye and one brown eye, both fixed on me as her newest target. Sadie wriggled in Everett's arms, as she attempted to close the gap between us to sniff me. "Why didn't you tell me you had a dog?" I held out my hand to let her get a good whiff, and she immediately started licking me.

"Well at first it was because I don't normally share personal details with my clients." He smirked, flashing his dimple at me. "Then after that I don't know...it just never really came up I guess? She stays with Meagan while I'm working, so I don't have to board her somewhere. Meagan can keep her upstairs though if you think it'll be too much for you." He looked at me, concerned.

"Don't you dare send her away." I rolled my eyes, leaning in to give Sadie some head scratches. "She couldn't possibly be too much for me."

"She's a failed emotional support dog," Meagan told me with a grin. "We wanted to get Everett a companion when he got back from the army, but it turns out that actual support animals are super expensive and take a long time to qualify for. So I looked online until I found Sadie, and got her at a discount."

"How did she fail as a support dog?" I rasped, as Sadie licked at my face.

"Support dogs are supposed to help with anxiety and PTSD-related issues by noticing their owner's distress and helping them to calm down," Everett explained, giving Sadie a scratch on the head. "Sadie here gets so excited to do the job, she'll end up tackling you, or sometimes head-butting. She means well, but it's hard to calm down from an anxiety attack after your support dog gives you a bloody nose." Sadie wagged her tail, her whole butt wiggling in Everett's arms.

Meagan laughed, hanging the leash up on the hook by the door. "Alright, I'll see you three later." She winked at me before disappearing out the door.

Everett set Sadie down, and she immediately started running circles around my legs, pushing against my shins. I wobbled, feeling myself being pushed over towards the couch. "Ya...she does that." Everett mused. "She's a herding breed, and they can be....pushy." I coughed a laugh and let Sadie herd me to the couch. As soon as I sat down, she was up in my lap, mission successful. I buried my hands in her soft fur, enjoying the warmth of her tiny body. Everett leaned down and gave me a chaste peck on the cheek before busying himself around the apartment.

He had been very PG since the incident. At first, I figured it was the whole me-almost-dying thing, and of course, we'd been in the hospital, which was not the most romantic of locations. But now I was starting to worry if maybe the spark I'd felt - that I thought we'd both felt - had fizzled out for him. Maybe he was just being sweet and biding his time until his week of babysitting was up, then he could more easily break it off and we would part ways like it was any other job. I felt a pang of sadness in my chest, and Sadie gave a low whine her head resting on my lap.

Everett made us dinner that night, which for me was a lovely broth and a protein shake normally given to old people who need to get more nutrients in their diet. My throat was no longer spasming every time I drank something, which was a nice improvement. I still couldn't help but glare at Everett jealously while he ate his delicious-looking sandwich. He made it up to me by producing two bowls of chocolate ice cream for dessert.

After dinner we watched a movie together on the couch, Sadie sprawled across both of us so she could get the maximum amount of cuddles. Everett eventually had to pause the movie when it became evident that I would not be able to stay awake for the end of it, and he ordered me to bed despite my protests. He'd even taken the time to arrange my pillow mountain on the bed, which was extremely thoughtful of him. I changed into a loose-necked shirt and some comfortable pyjama pants Layla had packed me, and climbed into bed. Sadie refused to leave the room, even when Everett tried to lure her with treats. I told him she could stay since she probably slept in here most nights and it wouldn't be fair to kick both of them out of their bed. Sadie happily curled up beside me, and her warmth was comforting in the unfamiliar room.

I lay awake for over an hour, staring at the ceiling of Everett's bedroom. Of course, now that I was actually in bed I couldn't get to sleep. My first night out of the hospital, and even though I was in what I knew was a safe place, I couldn't get my mind to rest. Slipping out of bed, I tiptoed down the hall into the living room. I caught Everett also lying awake, sprawled across his couch playing on his phone. He jolted up when he saw me, immediately concerned. "Are you okay? Is it your breathing? Should I call Dr. Schefield?"

"I'm okay, I just can't sleep," I whispered softly. I walked over to the couch and sat down on his lap, pressing my forehead against his. His arms drew around my waist, pulling me close. I heard his breath hitch as I settled my weight against his.

"What's wrong?" He breathed, one hand coming up to trace along my jaw. I brushed my nose against his, nuzzling him, wanting him to make a move and show me that my fears weren't justified. He made a soft noise in the back of his throat like a low growl, before cupping the back of my head and capturing my lips with his.

There it was. A spark of heat flickered to life in my core, and I parted my lips, darting out my tongue to deepen the kiss. He groaned into my mouth, his hand tightening on my side as I explored his mouth with my tongue. I could feel his body responding to my touch. I wanted more of him - all of him - I wrapped my arms around his neck, pulling him closer.

"Kacey, you're killing me." Everett groaned, the hand tangled in my hair pulling back gently until our face no longer touched. My cheeks were flushed, and I was gasping as air struggled to reach my lungs. "You're supposed to be resting, remember? No activities that get your heart rate up or that could make you short of breath."

"Then just give me mouth to mouth." I panted, and he laughed as I leaned in to kiss him again. He was right though, after another minute I pulled away, literally breathless, my chest tightening with panic. Everett held me while I struggled to catch my breath, rubbing my back gently while tears of frustration formed in my eyes.

"You need to get some sleep." He murmured, brushing a strand of hair out of my eyes. I pouted, and he chuckled.

"Can you stay with me?" I asked hoarsely, I knew I wouldn't be able to sleep unless he was nearby.

Everett scooped me up in his arms as he stood, and I wrapped my arms around his neck to keep from falling. "As you wish." He smiled, carrying me back to his room. It wasn't exactly how I'd imagined the night ended but curled up in bed with Everett to my left and Sadie's tiny form pressed against my right made me feel safe enough to finally drift off to sleep.

Chapter 29

Everett

Kacey was a terrible patient, she had no clue how to just sit and rest. Keeping her cooped up in my apartment was like sticking a jungle cat in a cage, someone was bound to get mauled. She stalked around the living room and paced up and down the hall with Sadie at her heels - who probably thought it was some kind of weird game. I tried to entertain her, putting on movies, and offering books, but she had this undercurrent of restless energy that just wouldn't dissipate. We couldn't really talk too much without it straining her throat, and other things - like what she'd started the other night - were off the table for similar reasons. I could tell she was frustrated - in more than one way - but I didn't know what I could do to cheer her up. She just needed to heal, and that would take time. And after she was healed....what then?

I wasn't technically on the job anymore. In fact, the job had ended the night I had killed her stalker, as per the contract Alexis had signed. But there was no way I was just going to abandon her in the hospital and move on to the next job. Instead, I put an Out of Office response on the email and phone systems and gave Jaime the week off, taking some much-needed personal time to take care of her. I wasn't sure if Kacey knew that though, and we hadn't really discussed what would happen now that she was safe to resume her normal life. We were stuck in this weird limbo, neither one of us saying what needed to be said.

I knew what I wanted. I knew as I watched Kacey standing in my kitchen wearing one of my tee-shirts as a dress, trying to get Sadie to sit for a treat. I knew when I noticed she was still wearing the fake engagement ring that Meagan had lent her, even though we no longer needed to pretend. I knew that I wanted Kacey. But what I didn't know is what *she* wanted.

By the fifth day of being stuck in my apartment, I came up with a plan that would give us both something to do. It was starting to get tense in the apartment, and I was worried Kacey was actually starting to go crazy, especially after I caught her trying to paint Sadie's nails.

"Where are we going?" Kacey asked for probably the fourth time, eyeing me suspiciously. We'd dropped Sadie off at Meagan's place and were now driving to our destination, which I still hadn't shared with her.

"You just have to trust me." I smiled, earning myself a dirty look as she huffed in frustration. Her voice was sounding stronger already, and she'd downgraded to only one pillow to sleep at night, which was progress, but I knew she still felt like it was taking too long.

I pulled up to the familiar building, and Kacey's face flashed a mix of emotions. "Oh." She sighed quietly.

As she got out of the car, I ran around to the trunk to grab the supplies. She looked confusedly at the stack of flattened cardboard boxes I pulled out, hoisting them under my arm.

"Come on, let's go pack up your things," I announced, heading inside.

"I still haven't decided if I'm moving yet." She called after me, her voice gravelly, like a hardened smoker's. She buzzed us up to our floor and slipped ahead of me to unlock the door.

"Well then, let's decide now," I replied evenly, following her inside. She stood quietly, staring into the condo, her face a confused mix of emotions. I gave her a moment to herself while I flicked on the lights and started assembling a few of the boxes, grabbing the roll of tape out of my back pocket. I watched Kacey out of the corner of my eye as she wandered over to the wall of windows, and I wondered if she was trying to see the other apartment from up here. When she didn't move for several minutes, I finally joined her, wrapping my arms around her from behind.

"I haven't even started looking for a new place yet," Kacey told me quietly. That told me all I needed to know.

"It's fine, you can stay at my place while you look. I've got a storage area where we can put your furniture." I kissed the top of her head, and she twisted around to look at me, her eyes red.

"I can't do that." Kacey insisted. "I've already put you out this week. And who knows how long it will be before I find a new place? I can't ask you to just upend your life like that." She bit her lip, looking down at the floor.

"Sure you can, and you can stay as long as you like." I smiled. "All I know is that I prefer my life when you're in it." Her cheeks flushed, and I desperately wanted to finish our non-conversation from the couch earlier this week. But Kacey was still healing, so I settled for giving her a gentle kiss. I pulled away before she could get any ideas, especially since I didn't think my self-control could hold out much longer. Kacey looked flustered and frustrated, but a small smile was tugging at the corners of her lips. "Come on, you can pack up the stuff you want to bring home today, and we can work on the rest tomorrow," I told her.

Home, I liked the sound of that.

I handed her a completed box and she set off towards her bedroom, still looking slightly irritated with me. When Kacey came out a while later, she had shed her hoodie and was now wearing only a thin tank top. She grabbed another box, ignoring me as she headed back to her room. When she returned for another box, still ignoring me apparently, I noticed she had taken off her sweatpants as well, now wearing only a lacy pair of panties. I busied myself with constructing more boxes, but I could feel my dick started to press painfully against my jeans. She was doing this on purpose, tormenting me as punishment for trying to let her rest and heal.

I was taking a water break when Kacey came back out, nearly choking when she walked past, her breasts completely exposed - just like the first time we'd met. She grabbed another box from the pile

I'd constructed, then stopped in front of me, grabbing my forgotten glass out of my hand. She finished my water in three sips, handing me the empty glass back before continuing on back to her room. I groaned softly, staring at her ass as she walked away, barely covered by the see-through pink lace. She was torturing me, and I didn't know how much more I could take.

I tried to clear my mind and set about dismantling the security system so I could bring the cameras back to the office. I sat down on the couch with my work computer and began deleting the old files and wiping the drives so they could be reused for a future job.

"Do you have extra closet space?" Kacey asked, startling me. I hadn't seen her come around the couch. I looked up to find her stark naked, arms crossed, a small smirk on her face.

"I...uh...what?" I stammered, my brain beginning to short-circuit. I half-expected smoke to start pouring out my ears at any moment. Kacey picked up my laptop and set it down on the table before taking its place, her arms wrapping around my neck as she straddled me.

"I have a lot of clothes. I'll need a place to put them." She smiled, fingers toying lightly with my hair. I knew she could feel what she was doing to me, and she seemed to be enjoying the torture.

"You can have my closet," I told her, and pressed my palms against my eyes, leaning my head back as she wriggled her ass, pressing down on my erection.

"That's very generous." She smiled, and grabbed one of my hands off my face, playing with my fingers. "But where will you put your clothes then?" She asked, and stuck one of my fingers in her mouth, sucking the length teasingly before nipping the tip with her teeth.

"Fuck I don't care, just throw them out." I groaned, my jeans painfully tight. Kacey's cheeks were flushed - clearly enjoying my discomfort. Her eyes sparkled mischievously as she placed my hand on her breast, her nipple hard beneath my palm. If she kept this up, I was going to come apart in my jeans like some high-schooler playing Seven Minutes in Heaven.

"This is cruel." I bit out, and Kacey rolled her hips once more, the pressure near agony on my throbbing cock. "I'm just following your doctor's orders." She tugged on my shirt, pulling it over my head and tossing it behind the couch. her lips blazed a trail of heat along my neck as she ran her nails down my chest, just hard enough to make me shiver.

"Good for you." Kacey smiled. "You can rest all you want." She reached down and unbuttoned my jeans, sliding them down my legs, my boxers following shortly after. The brief release of pressure was a short mercy, and I grabbed her hips as she rocked forward, rubbing her slick pussy against my cock. She paused, hovering herself over it, an impish grin on her face. I moaned loudly as her tight pussy parted around my cock, my fingers digging into her hips as she slid down at an agonizingly slow speed, taking every inch of me until I was buried in her completely.

Kacey hummed with pleasure and closed her eyes as she rolled her hips, using my cock to satisfy herself. I watched her for any sign that she was having trouble getting air in her lungs, but as her lips parted and she let out a soft moan, it was only me who stopped breathing. "Fuck it," I growled, and palmed her breasts, rolling her nipples between my fingers and she rocked against me. She moaned again and arched into my hands, her eyes snapping open to stare into mine, flushed with pleasure at her victory.

I grabbed her hips again and lifted her off my lap, Kacey squeaking in surprise. I set her back down on her knees and climbed up behind her on the couch, pushing her back down firmly until her forearms were resting on the arm of the couch. I thrust into her without hesitation, burying myself in her until my thighs pressed up against her ass. Pinning her by her hips, I continued to thrust, increasing my speed until she was moaning, her hands gripping the side of the couch. I wasn't going to last much longer at this rate, so I moved a hand down to tease her clit with my fingers. I rubbed at the sensitive nub until I could feel her pussy begin to spasm around me, then I increased the pressure, rolling it between my fingers until she cried out hoarsely, clamping down around me. I continued to milk her orgasm as my own crested, and I came inside her with a yell of my own.

Wrapping my arms around her, I pulled her against my chest and sat us back on the couch, cradling her in my lap. Her breath was coming in short pants, but it was nothing like before. I was amazed at how much she'd healed in only a week's time.

"Feeling better now?" I asked her gently, and she laughed, poking my nose. I leaned back until I was lying down on the couch with Kacey lying on top of me. I reached up and brushed a strand of hair back behind her ear.

"I think I love you," Kacey murmured, running her fingers over my eyebrow, gently avoiding the remaining stitches, which were holding together despite my recent face-plant. I smiled and kissed her as she blushed.

"I think I love you too." I laughed, holding her tight against me. The air around us felt lighter now that everything had been settled. Kacey would move, and she would stay with me until she found a new place, if she even needed one. Maybe we could find a bigger place together, close to a park for Sadie and driving distance from my office. I'd mention that to her later, it wasn't something we needed to think about just yet. I was just happy that she was in my arms, and that we were finally comfortable again after the chaos of the last couple of weeks. Everything had been figured out, and now we could finally relax and enjoy our time together. As soon as we were both healed up enough to face the public without scaring anyone, I would take her out to the nicest restaurant I could find, and we could finally have our first real date.

We both froze when we heard a noise at the front door. I rolled us over, lowering her down on the couch so I could slip off onto the floor, grabbing my boxers off the floor quickly. "Stay down," I whispered, pulling them on as I crept into the kitchen. The door handle jiggled impatiently, and I grabbed a knife from the knife block, rounding the corner just as the door swung open.

An older woman strode into the condo, pausing when she caught sight of me. "Well then." She murmured, her eyes scanning up and down. "I'm looking for my daughter, Katerina." She announced finally, and my chest seized. I shifted out of the fighting stance I'd taken, trying as best I could to cover myself, and wishing I could just sink through the floor.

"I'm Augustina Keeper." She told me, cooly. "I'm a little out of the loop I'm afraid, my daughter is not the most forthcoming when it comes to details about her personal life. You must be the bodyguard, or should I say fiancé, rather?"

Oh right, I'd forgotten about that. Fuck, so maybe not everything was figured out just yet.

Milton Keynes UK
Ingram Content Group UK Ltd.
UKHW040802291223
435170UK00001B/70